PENNINGTON FAMILY Book 2

KATHI S. BARTON

This is a work of fiction. Names, characters, places, and incidents are products of the author's imagination or are used fictitiously and are not to be construed as real. Any resemblance to actual events, locations, organizations, or persons, living or dead, is entirely coincidental.

World Castle Publishing, LLC
Pensacola, Florida
Copyright © 2026 Kathi S. Barton
Hardback ISBN: 9798245091563
Paperback ISBN: 9798891265103
eBook ISBN: 9798891265110
First Edition World Castle Publishing, LLC, February 16, 2026
http://www.worldcastlepublishing.com
Cover: Cover Designs by Karen
Editor: Karen Fuller

Chapter 1

Wylie was beginning to see the end of the construction of his house. He'd bought it because he knew he needed someplace to stay and hadn't thought of how much he'd hate the place. It was the hallway that he disliked the most. It didn't seem to have a reason for being there other than to divide the living room from the dining room. Plus, he'd had the kitchen upgraded, and that had needed it a great deal. Now it was beginning to look like a house that he could live in. But he'd not. He was going to get him something that he loved from the start and rent out the one that he'd so hastily purchased when the farm sold.

He and his brothers had sold off five thousand acres of prime land that went across several states to a man by the name of David Winchester. He'd not only given them a great deal, but he'd made millionaires of all six of them in the process. They were learning how to be rich men; it wasn't easy, and learn how to not lose their shirts in the process. It was something that he was learning daily, being around David and his wife, Alice. They were billionaires themselves.

"Did you learn anything about load-bearing

walls when the construction company was at your house?" He asked his brother, Gleason, what he wanted to know. "I was looking at this house, and the dining room and living room are across from one another like yours was. But the kitchen is in between. I want to open the dining room and kitchen up so that it's one big room. Otherwise, I don't like it."

"Then keep looking. If you have to figure out a way like that to like the house, then keep looking. You're in no hurry, are you?" He said that he wasn't so long as Kinsey and Meggie didn't kick him out. "They won't. I think they love having us all under one roof for now. Especially with Kinsey getting around better."

The accident that the two of them were in had nearly killed them both. Had they been in a newer truck than the old one they had been in, they would have been killed when a semi behind them had run them up and under a semi in front of them. Kinsey had been hurt the worst and had been in the hospital for a month before he could get around at home. He still couldn't drive yet, as it scared him a bit, but Wylie had gotten a car to drive and had been doing all right.

"I'm not finding anything that I want to live in. I know that I could build, but it seems to take a long time for them to get finished. I want something of my own now." He asked him about a condo. "I don't think I could live with people living right up in my face. I'm more of a loner than I thought. It's nice living with Kinsey and Meggie, they're great, but I do want something of my own to buy and live in."

"Then buy the house that you were talking about and fix it up. That way, you can get a feel for the construction part of your home buying and have a rental too. That's what I decided to do. I've bought the land, and construction will start as soon as I can find a house that I like. I figured that I can live in the rental when it's finished and then get a feel for living alone at the same time." He asked if he thought that he could do it after being with family all this time. "Yes. Because I know that you guys are only a few minutes away. Even if you only live in a condo or something else. I'm going to be visiting you guys all the time."

"I think I'm going to do it then. I've been looking at land that's out near where Kinsey lives. There's a lot of land for sale out that way. I'm going to get myself about ten acres and build. That way I can pick out the stuff that I want in a house while it's being put together." They hugged and then hugged again. "Thanks. I didn't know that I needed that until just now. Want to go and look at the house with me? I've been dicking around with it for the past three weeks, and I think that the realtor is getting sick of me asking to see it. But I want to make sure that it's right for me. But you've made me realize that it doesn't have to be perfect for me this time. I can just keep looking with having rentals in my wake."

"That won't be so bad either. Having income will make you feel better about having to find a house. I know that it does me. Just knowing that I'm going to be renting out the house I'm living in right now makes having to look for a place for my forever home easier. When they start on the kitchen, I'm going to have to rent something. I don't want to be in that kind of construction. Also, I don't have to rush into anything." Gleason said that made sense to him, too. "Let's go and see your house then. I'm thinking that it might not be as bad as you think."

"No, it's not bad. Just the rooms to the dining room and kitchen are too small. I want them to be opened up so that we can gather in the kitchen before eating dinner like we did at the other house. It was nice to be able to slide from room to room." Wylie told him that he'd liked that as well. "It made cleaning up better, too, because we could see what still had to be done."

They talked about the old farmstead that they'd been living in all together with their grandparents. Their father was in prison for killing their momma when she'd been at home with the six of them. Father was in for life without parole, which made it nicer for the six of them in not having to worry about him being around all the time. He could screw up a bad dream if he was around and none of them had anything to do with him since he'd been put away.

He loved Gleason's home. It was in a good neighborhood that seemed to be one where they took care of their homes. The kitchen was small. The dining room could fit a nice-sized table in it with lots of room left over, and he could see why he'd want to open up the space. It would be perfect for a home with lots of family over. They talked about how they would open up the front of the house too to be more welcoming, and before he left, Gleason made an offer on the house. He was sort of jealous about his first home being nearly perfect, but he'd find his forever home, or he'd build it. He was already getting ideas from his brothers' homes so that he could have the perfect home on the second try. Laughing to himself, he thought that Gleason was going to have the best house out of the rest of them because he'd taken his time with it. Just as he was going to do with all money decisions from now on.

They decided to get lunch at the local diner and were having fun when Raphael showed up. He said that he was finally finished working his trucking job and was free to get himself something to live in besides staying with his brother.

"I'm going to get a condo. I want to try living with people around. I've been alone most of my adult life and could use some interaction with people. Driving a truck for a living didn't leave me much room for a social life." They all agreed with him. "I've had my eye on this one that's on the corner of a lot with only one other person living next to me. I thought about buying them both so that I could have the rental income, but I'm not that far yet." He said that it sounded like a good plan. "My thoughts were that if I didn't like my neighbors, I could evict them and start over. That's my plan anyway. I don't know what I'd have done if not for Kinsey and Meggie letting me stay with them when I was off duty. I think I might have gone crazy living in the bed and breakfast for so long."

"I was thinking that, too." Gleason told Raphael how he'd put an offer in on a house. "This way, I can live there while the construction is going on and not be too bothered with it. I don't think. I need to get out on my own so that I can get my feet under me. Living with Kinsey is nice, but I think I'm getting lazy about finding myself a home to live in."

"I never thought of that." Both Gleason and he agreed that it was their problem too. They were making it too easy for them to get their own home. "It's like we're still living in the farmhouse together. I never thought of how it was making us do things. I'm going to move out this weekend."

"We can't all leave them at one time. They'll think we're not grateful for all that they've done for us. I'm going to be staying until I get the condo and get it cleaned up for myself. I'm going to tell them what I'm doing, but I'm not leaving until things are set up for me. I think we should all do that instead of living in construction zones all the time." Raphael had a good point, and he liked it. "I'm going to talk to them tonight when I get back for dinner and tell them what I've been thinking, not in a way that would hurt their feelings, but just to tell them how lazy I feel about the way that I'm doing things. I think they'll understand. Don't you?"

"I do. Meggie might cry; she's been sort of touchy lately with the tears all the time, but I think she'll be happy for us. Don't make her cry while I'm around. Her tears drive me crazy, and I want to just kill someone for making her do that." Both Gleason and Raphael agreed with him about making her cry. "Kinsey just looks foolish all the time, and I want to make fun of him. I don't. He's been lifting weights, and he's looking better than he ever has in the way of fitness. The doctor told him that had he not been in as good a shape as he'd been in, he might still be recovering from that accident. I was lucky that he tossed me under the dash, or I might still be hurting, too. His ankle is giving him the most fits. He has to use a cane still."

"I saw him this morning, and he was still using the cane. I hate to think about the accident. The way he looked and the truck looked afterwards. They said that had we been in a newer truck, one or both of us would have died." He shuddered when thinking about how lucky they'd been. "I'm just glad that we made it out alive. And for the most part, unharmed like we could have been."

"We all are." He thought about Rosie when he saw a cruiser go by. She'd asked him out the other week, and he'd had to turn her down. He'd had this function that he was required to go to about donations for the new school. He didn't know what to think about donations when they had tax money coming in from the sales of the land they'd sold. But it had been boring, and the food tasted stale like it had been cooked in the army of all things and brought to the dinner. He declined a date with her in order to be served stale food and boring company, and he'd regretted it ever since. What he should have done was take her with him. He would have at least had fun at the thing.

Rosie Donaldson and his brothers had gone to school together. She had been a couple of years younger than him, but they still were in some classes together in high school. She'd been so smart in school that he figured that she'd be married with about ten kids by now. So when she went to the police academy and finished at the top of her class, he'd not been surprised at all. What did surprise him was that she stayed in their little town and became the chief of police. No one had done a better job than she was doing for their town.

After leaving his brothers in order to get back to his house to see what was going on, he thought about her all the way to the police station. By the time he ended up there, he didn't know what he was going to say, but he knew that if he didn't ask her out, his head would explode. Seeing that she was in her office, she smiled at him and asked him what she could do for him.

"I was wondering if we could have dinner Friday night. I have one of those functions to go to, and I thought that if we ate before we had to be there, the food would be better." She burst out laughing, and he felt his face heat up. "I knew I was going to mess that up. I'm sorry. Would you go with me to this thing I have to go to on Friday? We don't have to call it a date if you'd rather not. I'm sorry for—"

"I'd love to have dinner with you Friday night. But I'm going to the same function with Ara. He asked me this morning." He wanted to cry. He'd finally worked up the nerve to ask her out, and she was dating his brother. Perhaps he could pound in his head so he couldn't go. While that had merit, he wouldn't do that to his own brother. "How about Saturday night? I don't have any plans, and I'd love to have dinner with you. I've had a crush on you since we've been in school together."

"Really?" She said that it might have started when he'd been in fifth grade and she in third. "That's a long time. And yes, Saturday night sounds perfect." They worked out the time he was going to pick her up, and she was agreeable to that. He nearly laughed out loud that it had taken him so long to get around to asking her out. "I should have taken you with me the other week. The thing was boring, and the food was terrible. But I sat through it all."

"I heard from the ladies who are friends with my mom how you were the hit of the night." His face heated up again, and he told her that he didn't know about that. "Mom said that the women were all over you. Made me sort of jealous about them."

"There was no need for that. They were all about twice my age, and while friendly enough, they were only talking about how I'd been part of selling the farm that we did. I think they were hoping I'd fund the entire school building, and that was it. I don't think that I'd ever be able to live it down if I were to do that."

~*~

Rosie had had so much fun at the charity ball last night. The men, both of them, were hanging out with her until Ara took her home. He'd been so sweet that when he'd kissed her on the cheek, telling her that he didn't feel right kissing her goodnight because of

Wylie, she found herself falling a bit in love with the younger man.

So tonight was her and Wylie's night to go out. She was so excited that she had to calm herself down several times before she could figure out what to wear. The dress she'd worn last night had been a last-minute decision, and she was glad that she'd gone with it. But tonight was special in that she was going with someone she'd been half in love with since she'd been just a little girl.

"Where are you going?" Surprised to see her mother at her door, she told her she was trying to decide what to wear. "Well, I think you should wear that black dress that you bought for vacation a couple of years ago. Knowing you the way that I do, you probably still have it hanging in your closet with the tags on it. Wear it and have some fun."

"It's a little too risky, don't you think? I mean, it's backless and not much more material in the front. It's just dinner. I'm not trying to seduce him." Her mom asked her why not. "*Mother!* It's our first date."

"I'm just pointing out that you've been in love with him forever, and this might be the only time you get to go out with him. Why not risk it all and go all out for it?" She had thought about the dress several times and always came up with the same thing. She'd not been trying to get laid by him. She just wanted a nice dinner with a good man. "It might do you some good to go out with him now that he's wealthy. I'm not saying that you could take him to the cleaners, but you'll have to admit, he can afford to take you just about anywhere you want to go."

"Now you sound like Candace at the bank. She said that she wanted to get knocked up by one of the Pennington men so that he'd build her a nice home that she could live in with all his money." Mom called her shameful. "I don't want to be one of those women who only see dollar signs when they go out with them. They're a nice group of men who just happen to be rich right now."

"You're right. I was wrong in telling you to wear something sexy. But if anyone deserves to be happy with a wealthy man, it's you. You've given up so much for your dad and me to have a retirement home that I don't know what I'd do without you." She said that she had the money and she could do it. "But to pay off the house for us was more than I ever expected you to do. You're the best daughter there ever was."

"Thanks, Mom. But I learned to be the best because I had the best parents in the world. You and Dad helped me get through college, and I'm forever going to be grateful to you." She decided to heed her mother's advice and have some fun tonight. Even if she didn't wear the little black dress, she had other dresses that made her feel good about herself. "I think I'm going to wear the blue one. If he's more dressed up than that, then I can always change. What do you think?"

"I think you have a brilliant mind and I'm proud of you." After her mom went to the living room, she got dressed. The blue dress wasn't nearly as revealing as the black one, but it fit her like a glove. And she felt pretty wearing it. When she heard the doorbell ring, she asked her mom to get it, and when she came to tell her that he had on a suit with a lovely blue tie that matched her dress perfectly. "Bring your cape with it. It's supposed to rain tonight, and you don't want to catch your death by getting a cold someplace you can't take medicine."

She told her she would, but didn't understand the part about medicine. Her mother had grown up with her grandparents around all the time, and she had picked up some of the strangest things to say. She'd hear herself saying the same things at times and wondered if people thought she was odd. Rosie shook her head at the nonsense in her head and picked up her blue shoes. She wasn't going down the stairs with them on where she might fall. She wanted to have fun, and being in the emergency department didn't sound all that pleasurable.

"I'll just be a minute." He was staring at her like

he'd never seen her before. "We're still on for tonight, correct?"

"Yes. I never realized how beautiful you were until this very moment. That dress is wonderful." Her face heated up, and she smiled at him. "I'm sorry, but you look so different than when you're wearing a uniform. It's not all that flattering, is it?"

"Not really. And that's a good thing, I think. No one hits on me because they think I have these large hips." They both laughed, and she kissed him on the cheek. "Thank you for the compliment. I feel so much better wearing this dress than something from the back of my closet."

"I'm sure from now on all I'm going to see is you in this dress. If you had worn anything else, I think I might have expired from your beauty." Smacking him gently on the arm, her mom said she'd lock up the house for her. "Thank you, Mrs. Donaldson. I appreciate your help."

When she got to the car and was helped in, she asked him what her mother had helped him with. He laughed and said he'd not got any ideas on what sort of food she liked from last night and wanted to impress her. Her mom had told him that she loved seafood and comfort food.

"I do love seafood. But I don't think there is anyplace around here to get that." He said he was taking her to Columbus to have dinner. "So far? Well, I'm not going to complain. I do love it and am happy that you asked."

They talked about different things on the way into town. There were all sorts of topics that the two of them could talk about, and she was still talking to him when they pulled up in front of the restaurant. She'd heard about this place but never expected to go there. Getting out of the car, Wylie pulled her into his arms and kissed her. Rosie held onto his shoulders as he made love to her mouth.

"What was that for?" He explained that he'd been wanting to kiss her since last night, but she'd been out with his brother. "Your brother didn't kiss me last night because he said that he could tell that I liked you better. Did you compare notes about dating me?"

"Nope. He didn't tell me that he didn't kiss you, only that he took you to the door and left. I thought that he'd take full advantage of you getting a kiss from a beautiful woman." She didn't say anything as he pulled her along to the front entrance. "I hope this is as good as they said it would be. When I asked for places to take you from Meggie and David, they said the same places. I'm glad you love seafood. It's one of my favorites as well."

Dinner was fun. They ate their fill with crab legs and baked potatoes. He had dessert while she had a cup of hot tea. It was the end to a perfect meal, she thought, and couldn't wait to see what else he had planned for them. It was still early enough that she didn't want to go home just yet.

They walked around the city block, and by the time they were back to the car, her feet were killing her. After getting in the car, she took her shoes off and apologized to him for doing so. He took her feet into his hands and massaged them before he even started the car. It felt glorious to have her feet done this way, and she moaned a few times when he got to the right places. Then her foot accidentally brushed against his cock.

Wylie didn't say anything, but he did stiffen a bit. After putting her feet back down on the floorboard, she couldn't even look at him. It wasn't until he said her name that she turned and looked at him with the light shining on his face from a streetlamp.

"I'm sorry." She asked him why he was sorry. "I tried not to get this way, hard you know, but with you making those little noises, all I could think about was what you'd say if I pulled you across my lap and made love to you for a bit."

"You mean necking a little?" He laughed and said that was a little tamer than he had in mind, but that was it. "We could go back to my place and neck if you want."

"What about your family? Would your mom have something to say about us making out in the car?" She said that she didn't live at home with her. "That sounds good."

"I would love that even better. But now that I think about it, we will be seen. I have a lot of nosy neighbors, and they'll actually come out of their homes to see what is taking me so long to get out of the car with you." He looked out the window and then back at her. "There's no hope for it. We have to find a dark space around here and make out. That's the only way that we can solve both our dilemmas."

"Our luck, we'd be arrested for indecent exposure. With you being a cop, it would be around town here and at home in no time. I guess we just go back to my place, have some fun, then I take you home. That's the only way that we can do this without anyone knowing." She asked him if he cared if anyone knew. "Not at all. But like I said, you being a cop, it wouldn't look good when elections came around again."

"There will be talk no matter what we do. I think you should just take me home and kiss me at the door like a good date would. They'll know it's our first date, too. You know how small towns are?" He said that he did, very much so. "All right. I could have been fun for you, too. I want you to know that."

"We could have blown the doors right off this

sucker in no time." They talked about having sex all the way home. It helped her, too, to know that he wanted her as much as she did him. "The next time we go out, we'll skip the meal and go straight for a hotel room. Out of town, of course. That way, none would be the wiser to our fun, and we can hold our heads up around there. What do you think?"

"I think we've given this way too much thought for our first date." Then she asked him if he wanted to see her again. He just stared at her. "I don't know your facial expressions right now. Perhaps you can tell me what you mean by that."

"I'm hard as stone and ready to lay you out on my seat to have you. I think that's answer enough, don't you?" She laughed, and he did too. It was fun being this free with their conversation. "I feel like I've been waiting for you all my life, love. Where have you been hiding?"

"I've been waiting for you to notice me at some point. I've loved you all my life, Wylie Pennington, and am so glad that we've been able to get together." He kissed her again and started the car. She forgot that they had to drive home now and wasn't looking forward to it. But he made her laugh, and that's all she wanted right now. "I do want you to come into my house. Damn the neighborhood. I'm a grown-assed woman who knows what she wants out of life. And you're it. It might not last forever, but I'll take what I can get from you. What do you say?"

"I love the way your mind works." They talked about their childhood on the way home. Wylie remembered a great deal about her as a child, and she'd been embarrassed about some of it, like the time he'd caught her watching him play basketball with his brothers. He and Raphael had gotten into a fight, and she'd defended him. "I never lived that down all summer. I always thought of you as a pest. You were sort of the way you hung around us all the time. I'm just glad that we were able to temper our language when you were around. There is no telling what your mom would have said about us with you hanging around us all the time."

"I think she knew that I had this crush on you from about third grade. You were so tall then, and I remember thinking that if I were to ever get to kiss you, I'd need a ladder." They both laughed and were almost home. "My mom would be all right with you staying the night with me. She'd wonder why it took you so long."

It was still early when he got her home. Every one of her neighbors was out on their front porches enjoying the evening air. So Wylie took her up to her door, kissed her goodnight, and left her there. So much for being a grown-assed woman, she thought as she went indoors all alone.

Chapter 2

Wylie was enjoying the classes. He was ready to invest in something online so that he could double his money. Laughing to himself, he thought that he'd more than likely lose his shirt than double his cash. But he was enjoying learning how to invest his money in things and get a profit from it. Now all he had to do was watch one of the many investment portfolios that he'd been told about and decide how much he wanted to put towards it. He wondered if he'd be ready for something like that.

"I've been watching two of the ones we were told about. I'm going to buy shares so that I can get started." He asked Kinsey if he was ready to do that. "I don't know why not. We've been taking classes for a month and a half now. We'd better be doing something with our money. Plus, I've been getting with David, and he's told me several things that he is watching. I know what that means, but I'm still nervous about putting some money on something that's not a sure thing. But we have to start someplace."

"I agree. Just where?" The six of them had been taking classes on how to be wealthy for two months.

Some of them had to do with investments, others were a simple thing like learning to have a conversation with wealthy people. That part wasn't so hard, but he still didn't know how to start a conversation with someone yet. He was better at talking about how poor he'd been. But no one wanted to hear that. "I feel like I'm not getting anything from these classes. What about you?"

"I'm learning a great deal. Have I used it yet is the question. I've not, in the event you were going to ask me. I've not found myself in a situation where I might have to talk about stocks. I think I can hold my own, but that's not saying much. Also, the class we had on eating in a formal setting was helpful. I would have screwed that up badly had I had to eat with all that silverware." They'd been teasing one another for the past several days. "I still don't know what to eat my ice cream with. Last night I ate it standing in front of the fridge, right out of the container. And the ice cream didn't care that I was barefooted too."

"It's like we're taking classes for dummies. I know how to eat a meal when I want one; it's not embarrassing myself that gets me. How the hell can I avoid eating with a bunch of people I don't know so that I can eat with my forks I know and understand?" Kinsey agreed with him, going so far as to say that he'd just as soon eat at home, too, the food was too odd.

"When they say we're having tiny plates, I expected them to bring out a tray of them for each of us. I can't be that hungry again and not have some food in my belly. I'm eating before I go out to dinner so that I don't sit there with my belly growling all the time. Meggie teases me, but she agrees that we should have a meal before going to dinner with some of these people. I think she's learning how not to eat as well."

They'd been having fun at the eating classes. The woman who was helping them was a Dame. Her house was large enough to accommodate them all, and she was helping them, but she would get frustrated too with how very little they were able to use the things that they were learning. She said she was going to have to have a party just so she could see how well her teachings had worked. Wylie didn't know what he'd do if he had to eat and talk at the same time. He was the most nervous of all of them about screwing up things.

He really didn't think that he would. He'd been paying attention in the classes, but he did enjoy the wine tasting parties that he'd been to. They were kind of fun in that everyone drank enough to get lightheaded, then they'd talk about how much the wine would go with certain foods. He'd had a cheeseburger the other night and wine to go with it. Yes, he was having fun in the classes like the rest of them were.

Walking into town when the classes were over, he'd have a bit to eat at the Dairy Mart in town. The food wasn't the greatest, but it was warm and filling. He was having himself a hot chicken sandwich when Bodi sat down next to him. He asked him what was going on.

"I've been looking at houses, and I'm going to build. Once I find a house that I like, I walk through it again after seeing it the first time, trying to imagine myself living in it. Most of the time, the kitchens need to be redone badly, and I don't care for the carpet that is in most of the rooms. Especially one with a fireplace. Have you ever noticed how there are burn marks on the carpet in front of the fireplace? Some of them are really bad, too. Like they tried to set the house on fire." He told him he'd never noticed that before. "I notice all kinds of things. I've been through David's house several times a day just to see how the construction is going, and it's wonderful to see a home go up from just a few boards in the ground to a large house. And his house is going to be large too when it's finished."

When Bodi ordered too, the two of them sat waiting for their food, talking about how Kinsey and Meggie were living in the most perfect house. How the kitchen is now up to date, and they love everything about it.

"I'd love to have a house ready-made for me.

I have been looking at blueprints. It's taken me some time to figure out how to read them, but I think I'm getting it now. Have you gotten that far in building a home?" He said that he'd not, but he would like to learn. "I can help you. I've been speaking with the construction crew at David's house, and they've been really nice in giving me advice. Some of the things that David is having put in his house are warmed floors for the winter months. I love that idea."

"I like that too. Warm floors are something that I could get used to. And a towel warmer. I've seen those online when I'm looking at houses. You should have a large bathroom too, Wylie. One that has several shower sprays so it hits you everywhere." They talked about silly things they wanted in their homes when their food was ready.

They ate in comfortable silence for a little while and enjoyed each other's company too. Bodi was someone who didn't have to be talking all the time, and Wylie loved that about him. When they finished eating, they talked about staff. It was something that no one had spoken to them about, but Kinsey had. They weren't in the way or anything and seemed to make the house seem cleaner all the time.

"I think I'd like to have someone come in and dust all the time. Also a cook." They agreed on the cook but not the dusting part. "Have you seen a speck of dust anywhere in their home? I mean, not even any dust bunnies under the bed when I lose a sock. And having the laundry done up by someone surely does make it better for us having to do it. I know you have to pay for all that stuff, but they surely do make things easier for you."

"But Meggie was used to that sort of thing before, and she works some. I bet she likes coming home to a clean house every day. I know that I would if I were her." They did agree on that. Meggie was good at being wealthy. "I've learned a lot from her, too. All kidding aside. She is good at having a meal with all of us, but I watch what she does when she's finished. You can't teach that to new wealth. That comes from having someone drill it into your head from being an infant."

They spoke about having dinner parties and going to them. He didn't think that Rosie would enjoy going to a dinner party with him. He knew that he was stiff at them, and it wouldn't be fair of him to invite her to something that he didn't care for. However, she might make it fun, he thought. He'd love to see her all dressed up again. Almost as if she knew he was thinking about her, she pulled up in front of the little diner in her cruiser. She'd been looking for Bodi.

"Did you quit working for Ralph's gas station the other day, Bodi?" He said that he'd given him a month's notice and had worked that and beyond. "He's telling people that you got too good to work for him and now you're planning on opening a gas station to run him out of business. I don't care one way or the other, but there is some powerful meanness coming out of some of the people who believe him."

"Why would I do that to him? He's a good guy. I just got tired of working all the time, and he was not looking for anyone to replace me. I have things I have to do now." She said that she believed him but wanted to give him a heads-up. "Thanks for that. But I have no intentions of owning another gas station. As far as I can see, Ralph's is a good place to get some work done on your car and fill it up, too. If you see anyone or they ask, I'm not going to be doing anything like that."

"I understand. He's just lonely without you there all the time." Bodi said he could understand that, too, as he didn't have much in the way of business. "I just wanted to let you know about what's being said. No problem from me if you were, but he's got it in his head that he's going to be run out of business by you, and that's what he's saying."

"I'll talk to him again. I had to quit working because he was leaving me there all the time. I really do have other things that I have to do." Rosie said that she believed him and would spread the word around, too. "Thanks, Rosie. Sometimes I don't know what this town would do without you hanging around. You sure can nip a rumor in the bud when it comes up. Can't you?"

"It's my job to keep the peace." She looked at him and winked. "How about a second date, Wylie? I've been thinking of that new Mexican place in Zanesville. We could go there and get some food and have a picnic."

"I'd love that. Tomorrow night, all right? Bodi and I were just talking about having dinner tonight together." Bodi said that he could eat some Mexican food with them, and Rosie rolled her eyes. Apparently, Bodi was thick-headed because he was making plans to go with them tonight. He'd have to have a talk with his little brother. "Bodi, she asked me out, not you. You and I can go out tonight, but I'm saving myself for the pretty officer for tomorrow night."

"I see how you are. You don't want me messing with your date." Bodi laughed. "I get it. I wouldn't want a third wheel around either if I were dating a pretty lady, officer or not." Bodi got up to take the trash away, leaving the two of them alone.

"Are we really going to have Mexican?" Rosie said they were going to pick some up and have it at her house. They could do whatever he wanted after that. "Anything? I mean, that leaves a lot open for me. I could use some more foot massages. Or whatever else you need. I've been thinking a great deal about you."

"I have you too. I want to see you again if you don't mind. The first date was just a teaser, I believe. We can have some fun watching a movie and eating, then you could stay the night. I'm not kidding when I tell you, you've been in my thoughts a great deal lately." He had to adjust his cock again for the hundredth time since he had been out with her. She was all he thought about as well. "Well, I have to go. I'll see you tomorrow night. I'll get with you on what I want to eat from there. They've brought in some menus that we can use, and I think that will be the way to go for us. Just bring it to my house, and I'll have drinks."

"No wine." She said she'd have beer like any normal person would have with Mexican food, and he laughed. "I'm still trying to decide if I like it or not. So far, the only thing I like is popping the cork from a bottle. I don't care for the taste at all on most of them."

"All right. I'll see you at six tomorrow night. I'll let you know what I want to eat." After she left him, Bodi came back with two ice cream cones. After being handed one, Bodi asked if he was serious about dating Rosie.

"I am. Do you object?" He said that he'd been thinking of asking her out as they were the same age, but he'd not now. "I appreciate that. We don't know where this is going to lead, but I'm thinking we could become serious sometime soon. She's been in love with me since we were kids."

"Tell me that you knew that, and she didn't have to point it out to you." He said that she'd told him. "I hope that I'm not that dense when I find a girl I want to date. Everyone could see that she's in love with you since high school."

After finishing their cones, they decided to go back to the courthouse and listen in on the rest of the classes that had to do with investments. He was willing to try to invest in something, but he wanted a sure thing. Bodi was the chance taker. He looked for him to be invested in all kinds of safe and not-so-safe things soon. Wylie wasn't a risk-taker at all.

~*~

Rosie was excited to be going out with Wylie again. She hoped that he had a talk with Bodi about the food they were having at her house and that he'd not be joining him. She liked the man a great deal, but not enough to have him around as a third wheel like he'd mentioned. Since it was going to be at her house, she didn't have to dress up so much and could wear her slippers. Her feet still ached a bit after walking around in heels that night. But she'd do it again if necessary. She wanted to be his date in all things that had to do with his new status as a wealthy man.

The money was his as far as she was concerned.

She didn't know how much he'd gotten in the deal, but he knew that he was several times over a millionaire. Kinsey was worth more because he'd married Meggie, and she'd been rich all her life. It was good to see them together, the two of them, and she was glad that they seemed so happy. She was that happy when she thought of Wylie.

Looking over the menu when she had time today, she settled on two different dinners instead of just the one she normally would have. If things went the way that she wanted them to, then they'd need to eat again sometime in the middle of the night. She wanted him in her bed and inside of her so badly she could barely sleep at night for thinking about him.

"Chief, there's a crowd developing at the Dairy Mart. Bodi is there trying to smooth over the people, but I don't think he's having much luck. Wylie and his brother are there too, and it's looking bad." She said she'd go back down there. "All right. I'll tag along, too, in the event you need something. Mr. Ralph is shouting about how Bodi quit working for him without notice."

"All right." She grabbed her gun and made her way to the car. If things got out of hand, she'd rather have the gun than not. As soon as she pulled up with her lights on, the crowd got louder. It took her shouting at them to get them to calm down. "I told you what was going on. What the hell are you doing bothering this man and his family when I told you up front he wasn't going to open a gas station?"

"He left me in a lurch. I don't have anyone working for me." Ralph looked ready to do battle, and all she had to do was put her hand on her gun. "You're not going to arrest him, are you? They get themselves a bit of money, and they don't want to help out their fellow man no more. I see how they are."

"I gave you notice, Mr. Ralph, but you kept asking me to stay a little longer. I worked for you for three months past the time that I said that I'd work for you. You never seemed to be looking for anyone to replace me." He said that wasn't true that he did look. "Mr. Waggoner said that he asked you several times for the job, and you kept telling him that you had enough people working for you. I had to do something, or I'd still be working for you. I needed to get out from under the station."

"I liked you being there. Now you're too good to work for me." He said that he had to have time of his own. "I don't want to hire anyone else. You was a good employee, and I liked you being there. What am I supposed to do now that you're gone?"

"Hire Mr. Waggoner. He's a good mechanic. Better than I was." Ralph said it wasn't the same. "Nothing is the same anymore. I want to have a good life for myself and find myself a wife to have a bunch of kids with. I can't do that and work for you fifty hours a week, plus the things that I have to do now. I'm going to build myself a house. Find me a wife and have some kids. Don't you think I should be able to do that?"

"I guess so." He looked around at the crowd that he'd gathered and told them to go home. He'd been upset with Bodi when he'd just quit him. He'd given his notice just fine, but he didn't want anyone to leave him while it was working out so well. "I fibbed a bit on everything. He's a good man and doesn't deserve what I'd said about him. I can't wait to see him with a wife and kids. He'll be a fine daddy just like he should be. Nothing like his own bastard of a father had been."

The crowd disbursed soon after, and Ralph told everyone he was sorry for what he'd said. Bodi said that he'd help him out when he could, but he couldn't work full-time. That he should hire Mr. Waggoner so that he'd have a good mechanic at the gas station to help with things that came in. After that, it was hard to believe that some of the people who had been there had been spitting mad at Bodi as they were all shaking his hand and patting him on the back. Small towns were like that. Easy to fire up and to knock the flames out at the same time.

Going back to the station house after talking to Wylie again, she was glad that she'd looked at the menu before leaving. He was going to get them some appetizers as well as their meals so that they could pig out as much as they wanted. She hoped that he was willing to stay the night. She'd been looking forward to it for so long to have sex with Wylie Pennington.

By the end of the day, she was ready for a nap. It had been a long one, too, with the crowd that had been at the Dairy Mart. However, she needed to get home and clean her place up for company. She'd even made plans to change her sheets on the bed so that they'd be fresh when he got there. As soon as she was home, she did take a bit of a nap and was ready to start on the house by six-thirty.

By ten that night, not only had she gotten her house cleaned up, but she'd also brewed some tea for the two of them. Beer was in the fridge, and she was happy that she'd been able to get a couple of different brands. She had wine too, but since he'd not liked it, she didn't even bother with opening it up for herself a glass.

Rosie was as ready as she could be for her second date with the love of her life. She really was in love with Wylie and had been forever, it seemed. She was going to make sure that he knew how much she was in love with him tomorrow night, too. While she didn't know if they'd ever marry or anything like that. She just wanted to be with him while she could. Not only was she in love with him, but she also thought that she could consider him a best friend too. They could talk about anything and everything when they were together.

Up by six the next morning, she'd not slept all that well; she'd changed the sheets on her bed and put the dirty ones in the washer. They'd be drying when he got there, but she didn't care. Things were about as perfect as she hoped they'd be, and she was glad that she'd be able to have him over tonight. Almost as soon as she was in the office, she knew it was going to be a longer day than she wanted.

Right off the bat, she was brought into a big fight with one of Mr. Ralph's neighbors. He was going to expand his place, and she didn't want the lights of his new place keeping her up at night. As far as she knew, there weren't any neighbors close enough to be bothered by extra lights, and she thought that the woman just wanted to complain about something. She was going to have to go and see the elderly man to see what was going on, and she wasn't looking forward to that. She'd just gotten him calmed down from before; she didn't want him to get his dander up again about someone complaining about lights that may or may not happen.

After getting that squared away, she had to work at keeping the town together. There were so many little fires that had to be put out, she sometimes felt like she was a school teacher and that her students were acting out again. As soon as lunch time rolled around, she was ready to call it a day. Lucky for her, she had Wylie to look forward to tonight and was excited as she'd ever been about a date.

By the time it was quitting time for her, she was ready. Going home, she was just putting her sweats on when the doorbell rang. Wylie had a lot of food with him, and she helped him carry it into her kitchen. She wondered what he'd gotten when he started naming off things that had been on the menu that he'd wanted to try.

"If we don't eat it all, we can eat it tomorrow. I'm not going anywhere tonight, so I'm planning on making love to you all night." She told him good that's what she needed and they laughed. "I'm feeling kind of like a man on Christmas morning. I have no idea why I feel that way, but it's a good feeling."

"I've been working hard all day and would find my mind drifting to you coming over, and I'd have to wake up my computer again and start to work. It's been a long day, and I'm looking forward to eating a nice, fun meal with you." They separated out the food and began opening the containers while they sampled each thing. By the time they'd gotten everything out of the large bags, she was ready to have a big meal and sat down at her table with Wylie to enjoy dinner. It was fun to have so much to choose from, and she was glad that he'd done it this way. She was stuffed by the end of the meal, and they didn't have as many leftovers as she'd thought they would. Skipping lunch today had made her very hungry.

Going to the living room, leaving the mess in the kitchen, they sat down on the couch to watch some television. She could see them doing this all the time, the two of them just enjoying each other's company. By the time she'd dozed off for the third time, she was ready for bed. Her belly was full, and she had a great man in her place. What more could she ask for than that?

At around midnight, she woke up to be entangled with Wylie on the couch. He was snoring softly, and she had her head on his chest. The sound of his heartbeat lured her to sleep again, and she didn't mind that she wasn't in bed with him. She was just where she needed to be, and she loved it.

Getting up at two, she had to go to the bathroom. He was lying on her in a way that she was smushed up under him. Getting off the couch, she was glad that she'd had to roll to the floor to get out from under him because had they been in bed, she would have hurt herself. Going to the bathroom and turning off some of the lights, she was startled to find him sitting on the side of the couch waiting for her.

"I guess we should go to bed. I'm more exhausted than I think I've ever been." She said that she'd had a long day as well. "We can sleep together tonight and make love all day tomorrow. How about that?"

"I think you have a wonderful mind." They laughed, and he took her hand into his as she led him to the bedroom. "I've been looking forward to this all day, and now I'm going to sleep with you. I don't care what people will think about your car being in the driveway all night, either. I'm fed up with living my life around others."

"That's kind of out there." She told him that she'd been thinking about quitting her job for a while now. "I can understand that. It must be hard on you to get up every day to clean up messes that have to do with people. I think I'm going to enjoy not having to work hard every day. I just want myself a nice house, a garden for the fresh things that I've gotten used to, and have a good life with you."

"What are you saying when you say that? I mean, we've only been out twice, and one of them was us sleeping on the couch." He said that he was in love with her. "I want you to be sure about that, Wylie. I've been in love with you since childhood, and if you break my heart, I'm going to be a shell of a woman from now on."

"I'm sure about what I'm saying. Today, when

I saw you there with the crowd of people, I knew that I wanted to spend the rest of my life with you." He got down on one knee and pulled out a little blue box. "I saw this, and I thought of you. It's going to be one of the many things that I buy you from now on because I want to pamper you for the rest of my life. Will you marry me, Rosie? I'm so in love with you that I find that I can't keep my heart in its place when I think of you."

"You have to be sure. I'm not going to say yes, then have you change your mind in a few months. If you're serious, then I am too. Yes, I'll marry you." They kissed and held each other. He'd not put the ring on her finger yet, and she found that she didn't care. She was going to spend the rest of her life with the man of her dreams, and she couldn't have been happier. Once he put the ring on her finger, she knew he'd spent a lot of time on picking it out. It was perfect for her, and she couldn't wait to tell her parents. After all this time, she was going to be married to the man of her dreams. Yes, she thought, life was just about as perfect as she'd ever dreamed it would be, and all because she'd found the man of her life.

Chapter 3

Wylie put the condoms on the bedside table and stripped off his pants. He wasn't rested enough to try and make love, but if she was willing, so was he. He'd never been so happy to be in love as he was tonight. He told himself it wasn't because he was being laid, it was making love to someone that he loved. Forever.

Getting into bed, he was under the covers before Rosie was, and felt good about that. He didn't want to have to strip down naked in front of her. He'd be embarrassed at how hard he was. And he was hard. When she came out of the bathroom, she was wearing an oversized shirt. It might well have been one of his; it was so large on her, but he knew better. He'd not been here long enough for her to have taken one of his shirts.

"I bought it. It doesn't belong to anyone I knew in the past." He'd not thought of that, but was glad that she'd told him. "I don't have any pajamas or anything like that. I find it more comfortable to sleep in old T-shirts. I hope I didn't upset you."

"No. To be honest, I never thought of that when I saw you in a shirt. I just knew that I hadn't left you one." She said she'd like it if he did when he left. "I can do that. Most of my clothes are old anyway."

When she got into bed with him, he tried to warm her up. Her entire body was chilled, and she was making him colder by getting close to him. Once she stopped shivering, he pulled her into his arms and held her. Her body was soft yet firm, and he loved the way she smelled, too.

"I've never had anyone here before. Usually, I go to a hotel when I want to have sex." He wasn't sure why she was telling him that, but paid attention. "I don't do one-night stands either. Up until about a year ago, I was seeing this guy for purely fun. We'd have sex on occasion, then go home. There was nothing really between us other than to get laid. We were friends with benefits, I guess you could call us. I babble when I'm nervous. Are you nervous?"

"I am now that I'm in bed with you. I'm not sure where to begin." That made her giggle, and he laughed with her. "I know what to do, I'm just not sure that I want to make love to you right now. I just like holding you for a bit."

"You're warm." He said it was because he'd been in bed longer than her. "I don't think that's it. You're really warm. Like cuddly warm. I love it." She moved closer, and he rolled to his back so that she could lay her head on his chest. "I love the sound of your heart beating. It's very soothing. I could get used to this."

As she laid there, he thought of all the things that he'd done to be here tonight. He'd told Kinsey where he was going and the plan, but none of the rest of them. He didn't want them to feel differently about Rosie if this didn't work out between them. He didn't know why, but that was his thought process when he'd decided not to tell them. Moving her hair off his chin, he wondered what it would be like to wake up with Rosie. Closing his eyes, he let himself drift off to sleep while holding onto her.

He didn't know what time it was when he woke up. The bed was a tangled mess, and he couldn't seem to figure out what was up or down. Bumping someone in the face, he was sorry as soon as she cried out. Hitting her in the nose wasn't what he'd meant to do, and he told her that.

"Well, I should hope you didn't mean to hit me." She told him to stop moving. "I thought my double bed would be big enough for the two of us, but obviously not." When she turned on the light, he fell out of bed trying to get away from it. Rosie started laughing as soon as he looked up at her. "This bed isn't big enough for the two of us, is it?"

"I have a king at home." He looked over the blankets and pillows that had been tossed off the bed.

"I'm thinking that we should have come to my house now. At least we'd both fit." He stood up and helped her remake the bed. "I'm truly sorry that I hit you. I didn't know where I was when I woke up. Like you, I don't do this often enough to be very good at it."

"I'm sure you were working too hard to form a relationship with anyone." He told her that it was right. "I'm glad that the two of us can get together to see if this works. I'm sure it will, and I will marry you, but we have some things to work out. I'll sign a pre-nup for you if that's what you want."

"I don't want that. What I have is yours, and what you have is yours too. I don't know how much you know about the sale, but I can tell you that we've all become millionaires overnight. It's a heady thing to realize sometimes." She told him that she'd never known a millionaire before. "Well, now you know a whole family of them. My brothers are all the same as me."

"I heard that Kinsey was the only one who owned all the land that your grandma left to you. It was great of him to share his millions with the five of you. I've also heard that he got the lion's share of the money. I don't know which to believe." He told her what had happened. "I thought as much. Kinsey is a good man, and he'd want to share it equally with the five of you. You're all good men, and I'm glad to have been around you all my life."

"I forget about that sometimes." They were finished making the bed now, and he sat on the edge of it while she got comfortable inside the covers. "I forgot that we all grew up around here together. It's nice to know that we've been friends for a long time and now we're going to get married. I couldn't ask for a better partner than you in my life."

"Thank you. I think so as well." She opened the covers, and he slid in beside her. The bed was cooler now, but he soon warmed up. When Rosie moved closer to him and snuggled under his chin, Wylie thought that he could live like this forever and not change a thing. "I'm exhausted, but I have to tell you how much I love you being in bed with me. It's like we've been doing this for a long time, like an old married couple. I love you, Wylie."

"And I love you." He was ready to close his eyes when he realized that he really was enjoying being in bed with her. It wasn't a frantic move to have sex but just to be with each other. He decided that other than a bigger bed, they could be like this forever. Just two people in love sleeping together. "Good night, Rosie."

"Good night, Wylie." She was asleep in just a few moments, and he found it easy to let sleep slide over him as well. He'd been looking forward to this for so long; he didn't want to mess things up by fumbling around in the dark to make love. The bed was too small, or he was too big for it, and he was content, for now, to be able to be with Rosie in a more personal way.

When he woke up the next time, the sun was shining through the windows. He was alone in the tiny bed and got up to find Rosie. He found her in the shower, washing her hair. Joining her, she handed him a netted sponge and asked him to wash her back. He was more than happy to oblige.

"I've never had anyone wash my back before. It feels really good." He said that he'd never washed anyone before and was enjoying her moans of appreciation. "Are you hard?"

"I am. I'd like nothing more than to press you against the wall here and plow you." He washed the back of her arms and then turned her around so that he could wash her front. Her nipples were hard as he was, and he leaned down to suckle one into his mouth. "Perfection, just as I thought it would be."

Pulling her toward him, he turned her around so that she could sit on the bench seat against the wall. Getting down on his knees in front of her, he opened her legs wide so that he could see her pussy. It was more than he thought he could stand in how beautiful she was.

"I'm going to eat you." She leaned back against the wall and pulled his head toward her while she smiled at him. "I want you in the worst sort of way, Rosie. I'm going to enjoy this."

"I am too." He moved between her legs and licked her from gate to clit. Taking the little morsel into his mouth, he nipped at her as he slid his finger into her sheath. She was warm and wet, and it had nothing to do with the fact that they were in the shower together. Rosie tasted of heaven and the sweetest fruit that he'd ever tasted.

When she pulled his head up from her, he wanted more of her. She told him she wanted him, and he realized they were going to have to go to the bedroom because he'd left his condoms there. She told him that she was on the pill and couldn't wait for him to fill her. Everything in his world seemed to have stopped moving at her husky request.

Picking her up, he pressed her against the shower wall and slid inside of her. She was hot and wet, and he realized that the shower had been turned off. While he took his time making love to her, she wrapped her legs around his hips and held onto him with her arms around his shoulders. Taking her mouth, he kissed her savagely because he wanted her to know how much he needed her.

When she clawed at his back with her nails, he came. Throwing back his head, he cried out that he was coming and knew that on some level, he was hurting her. As he came a second, then a third time, his body wasn't prepared for the way he felt coming as hard as he did, and had to lean his head against the wall so as not to fall on his ass. His breaths were coming out hard, and he was shocked that he didn't pass out. His body was spent in that moment, and he couldn't believe that he'd come so many times in a short amount of time. He knew that he was going to be sore but didn't care. He'd made love to the woman of his dreams, and he couldn't have been happier.

Turning on the shower again, he washed her back again. She told him that she'd cut into his back and was sorry for that. He told her that he'd think of them as badges of honor the way they'd made love.

"You're ridiculous." They washed each other's bodies and hair again. He was enjoying himself, washing parts of her that he'd touched. As soon as they were ready to get out, he told her that he was going to need another nap, and she laughed at him. "I didn't know you were such a lightweight. I'll have to go easier on you the next time we make love."

"You've no idea how long it's been since I've had sex. And I've never had it like we just did. I hope you don't make a habit of making love to me like that. I'll be old before my time if you do." She laughed, and he did as well. "I'm starving. How about we go and get us something to eat and then come back here and take a nap?"

"I'd love the first part, but I don't think we can take a proper nap with that bed. I should have thought of how big you were when I suggested that you come here to stay the night." He told her that they could go back to his place. "I'd love that idea. All right. Food and drink, I think I cried myself hoarse, then we'll go to your place and take a nap. I'm all for spending the day in bed with you."

As they were getting dressed, he couldn't help but touch her. Her skin was so soft that he found himself mesmerized by the way it felt. Even as they were headed down the stairs to the living room, he found that he wanted to touch her. Holding her hand when they went out to his car made him feel like he could have been king of the world.

They were too late for breakfast but settled on some burgers for lunch. He had two to her one, and he enjoyed most of her fries when she said she'd had enough. The milkshakes were fantastic, and he loved that she took his cherry off the top of his. He couldn't stand cherries in any way or form and was happy to be able to share them with her. As they were leaving the restaurant, he kissed her again and decided that he was going to do that every opportunity he got. He loved the way that she tasted, like chocolate milk he used to have as a kid when he was living with his mom.

They made it back to his place within the hour. She wanted some things to leave at his house, and he couldn't find fault with that. He smelled like her scents when he'd showered with her and decided that he'd get some things to leave at her home in the event that he stayed over again. Since he was house hunting, he decided that they were going to have a special bed made that would be big enough for the two of them when they made love. He didn't think that his king-sized bed would be big enough if they were going to be making love in it all the time.

"I have a couple of appointments tomorrow afternoon with the realtor. I'm going to be building, but she said it would be easier if I were to have what I want in mind before I decide anything." She said that she'd help him with the house, too. "You don't have to do that. I'm going to be putting it in both our names, but I really do have enough money to pay for us a house to be built. I already have a list of things that I want in it." He handed her his phone so that she could see his notes.

"I love the idea of warmed floors. And the bathroom having its own heat source is an excellent idea." She went over the list that he'd had and handed him back his phone. "The only thing that I would like is a nice big kitchen. I love having meals in there when I'm home. Are you thinking that we need a staff?"

"I want one or two people around to clean up after me. You know, dusting and stuff. I've seen what they can do when I was at Kinsey's home, and I love that they keep you straightened up." She asked about a cook. "I don't know what your plans are for working, but I'm going to have to find something to do to keep me from lazing about. I can cook, but I don't want to have to do that after working all day. I think a cook would be wonderful for that reason alone."

"I don't cook. I can, but I'd rather not. I don't much care for eating out every night, but I do get tired of fast food all the time." They talked about other staff as they laid down on his bed and what she wanted to do about her job. "I like my job, but I'm working too much right now. I think it's because I've been bored at home. I don't see that happening when we're together. I might have to work outside the home so that I can get some rest between bouts in the bed."

They both laughed, and he was glad that they could talk so easily. Who would have thought that a week ago, he was just looking for someone to fall in love with over time. He never realized that he was going to find her in the chief of police and a childhood buddy. Wylie was in love with his little cop and was glad that she loved him as well.

~*~

They added to their list of things that they wanted in

a house, but neither of them found a layout like they wanted. The houses were either too big for a couple right now, or they had too much wrong with them to even think about duplicating for their own home. They had plenty of time; he'd been living with Kinsey until recently, and now that he was in a condo, they had all the privacy they wanted. Rosie thought that house hunting was boring and didn't care if she looked at another house as long as she lived.

"We have one more to look at, then we'll call it a day." She wanted to beg him to stop, but knew that this was important to their lives together. He didn't want to be moving around again when the kids started coming — the thought of having kids with Wylie made her feel like a wonderful person, and she decided that if she were to get pregnant right now, it wouldn't bother her at all. But she did have Wylie keeping her from stopping taking the pill. They didn't have a house yet, and that would be important to them in the long run. "This one she saved for last because she thought that it would be the one that made us decide to buy instead of build."

"I hope so. My feet are killing me." She'd worn heels again and regretted it the moment that they'd stepped outside of the condo. "I should have listened to you about walking so much. You'd think that I wasn't used to walking on my feet all day, but it's the heels. I'm not used to that much walking in them."

"I'll give you a foot massage when we get back home." She perked up, thinking about where that might lead, and told him that she'd love that. "Good. I think when you make those little sounds of pleasure, I could take you right then and there. You're very vocal when you're happy, and it makes me happy when you are."

The house was nice. It had a great deal of charm about it, if not just a little too over the top in the decorations around the place. She wondered if it was a distraction from whatever they were hiding, but didn't want to go there. When she made her way into the kitchen, she fell in love with it. It was just what she imagined a large open kitchen to be like.

There was a sunroom that was off from the general cooking area that she loved. It was a table and four chairs that she could see them having a meal at any time of the day. She didn't even like to cook and could see herself making them a meal in the large room. Even the island in the middle was nice in that it had a sink and electrical outlets so that it could be used as an extension of the counters. Yes, she thought, this was a perfect kitchen layout.

The living room was huge, and she thought that she couldn't see them being comfortable in the room. But then she realized that his family would be over a great deal and wondered if the room was going to be large enough. Laughing to herself, she wondered if they liked sports on television and thought of a large television on the wall to accommodate the room size. She could see them spending a great deal of time in this room with his family around. It would be loud with laughter and shouting at whatever sports were on the television. There was even a fireplace big enough to warm the house that she fell in love with as well.

There were six bedrooms on the second floor that she loved, plus the master suite that had its own library as well as an office. There was a large bathroom in the suite, as well as a living room sort of area where the people had exercise equipment. She wouldn't do that, but make it a living space for the two of them.

There was also a full basement that doubled as a media room, where she could think of all kinds of things to do with it other than what they were using it for. Like a kid's room that would keep them happy and maintained. Not that she planned on tossing them down there and not ever being with them. She had grown up with her own space in the house and thought that any child would love that as well. She knew that she had.

"Well, what do you think about this house?" Wylie said he wasn't sure it wasn't too perfect. "I understand. I'm not supposed to tell you this, but they don't have any offers on the house. The rooms are too big for what most people want. The reason that I thought you'd like it was because I know you have a large family."

"Yes, there is that." She pointed out that the furnace was new and that the roof had only been put on about four years ago. "How hard is it to heat in the winter? I mean, with a fireplace that big, will it be necessary to have it going all the time?"

"You must not have noticed that it's gas. They had it converted to gas about five years ago to save on having to chop wood. And no, it's not hard to heat or to cool off in the summer months. There is a separate furnace and air conditioner for the second floor. And the master has its own heating. The bathroom has been upgraded with some of the things you mentioned. There are heated floors in the bathrooms, all of them, and there is a towel warmer in the master."

"I didn't see any of that on the paperwork." She said that she'd tried to tell them that they needed to add it, but they thought it should sell for what they see. "I guess their loss is our gain. When do you have to have a decision? I'm hoping that we can have at least tonight before we have to have an answer."

"Take your time. As I said, they don't have any offers on the house, and it's been on the market for four years now. They keep making improvements in hopes of selling it. As I said, it's been on the market for a good long time." They decided to have dinner and talk about it. "I'd only offer what you think it's worth. You know what you want in a house, and this one pretty much ticks off your list fully. But you know what you want, and that's the biggest factor in this home."

"We'll get back to you soon. I'm going to make a list of the pros and cons about it and go from there. But like you said, it does hit our lists fairly well." They were out in the car when they started talking about the house. "I love too that it has a pool and pool house. It wasn't on the list, but I can see where it will be nice for when the family comes over. I know that Kinsey has one too, but it's not as big as the one that we would have."

"I know that I said that I didn't want to cook, but that one makes me want to whip out a cookbook and go at it." He laughed with her. "I do love the big rooms. I didn't think I would at first, but then I thought of how big your family was and thought that it might be too small if they were all to come over at once. I love the living room for sports on television. Do you like sports?"

"Football. Soccer. Baseball. You name it, and I love it. I even love watching football in London. It's so different than ours." She told him that she'd watch just about anything as well. "Good, another thing that we have in common. I love that we can have so much in common and be friends as well. I think we're going to have a long and happy life together."

"I hope so too. I love you." He kissed her as soon as he started the car, and they were on their way to dinner. The two of them would point out things that they liked about the house and the few things that they didn't. The only thing that neither of them cared for was the front door. It should be a double door instead of just the single one that it was. "But it's fixable if we want to do that. The only thing that would be difficult to fix, if possible at all, is how far it is from your family. It's a good twenty-minute drive from the closest one to our house."

"So? They'll come no matter where we live, I think." She thought that was true and told him so. "So what kind of offer do we make on it? She said to go low, and I agree with her. I'm thinking that we should drop about twenty percent off the asking price and go from there. It sounds like they're willing to sell the place, and I'm willing to pay what we need within reason to own it. I think it'll be a good home for us and the family if you want to have one."

"Yes, I want to have several children with you. I don't know how many right now, but I'd love to have them soon." He kissed her again when they were at the stoplight. "I love that you do that. Show me how much you love me by the little things that you do."

"Because I love you." They drove into Columbus for dinner and had made plans to stop off at a couple of furniture stores to have a look around. They wouldn't buy anything right now; they didn't have a house to move into yet, but they could get some ideas on what they wanted. Wylie decided that having money to spend was wonderful in that they could get the whole house fitted out without any trouble. He wasn't going to go broke about it, but he was looking forward to having their own things around them as they moved in. "We'll need a larger than normal bed. I don't know that a king will be big enough for the two of us when we make love. And we're going to need something larger than a double for sure. I doubt that would work for any of my brothers, even without their other halves with them in it. It's just too narrow and not nearly long enough for any of us."

"I never thought of that when I invited you over." They ended up at another seafood restaurant and this time had some dessert that they shared. "I'm exhausted."

"I am as well. Now that I have my belly full, I feel like I need to go to bed and nap for about three days." She laughed and said she felt the same way. "We'll leave shopping for another day, after they accept our bid on the house. Then we will be able to measure and get what was needed for the house instead of just guessing."

"I think that instead of having chairs and a single couch in the living room, we should go with all couches. That way, everyone can have a seat, and they won't feel as overcrowded." He said he loved that idea. "Also, we need to make sure that we can extend our dining room table enough to make sure that we have enough room in the place. I'd hate for your family to be crowded in there when we're trying to eat."

He told her to make notes on that. As they were headed home after dinner, they discussed putting a bid on the house. Since they both liked it and had seen it now, they decided to go with the twenty percent less offer. All they could do was counteroffer, and they could decide whether they could do that. It was fun buying a house that he had put some thought into, and he told her that. As they were pulling into the driveway, she was nearly asleep.

Since it was early yet, he called the realtor and told them what they wanted. She said she would take them the offer tonight, and they might hear from them in the morning. Glad that part was over with, he decided that he was going to sleep good tonight and was glad that they were at the condominium he was renting. It was much nicer than her house, and the bed was big enough.

Chapter 4

Kinsey didn't think he cared for being rich. Before he had any money, it was easy to make decisions about things. He didn't have any money, and there was no point in speculating on whether or not they could afford something. He didn't know how people did it all the time and didn't go insane. He was driving himself crazy with making a decision on every little thing. He looked up from his computer when Meggie entered the room.

"How are you feeling? Still getting sick all day, I noticed." She said she was feeling better today, but that might be a one-time thing. "I'm sorry that you're sick all the time. If I could make you better, I would. But we're going to have a baby, and that makes it all worthwhile."

"I'm sick of being sick all the time, but the doctor said that I'm doing fine and the baby is too. I can live with a little sickness so long as the baby is fine. When do you want to tell your family? I'm thinking sooner rather than later, so they don't think that something else is wrong with me instead of being pregnant. Do you think they might have guessed what it is?" He said that he didn't think they'd figured it out, but he didn't know. "I'm going to tell my mom the next time I talk to her. She'll be thrilled, I think. I find that she's slightly annoying at times. But that could be just me. I don't have a lot of patience with people nowadays."

"I've noticed that you seem to be rolling your eyes a great deal. Not that I think anyone notices. But I do because I'm in love with you." She started to cry, and he came around the desk to be with her. "I'm sorry, love. I didn't mean to upset you again. Please tell me what it is that I can do for you, and I'll give it to you."

"Nothing. I'm just so touchy lately. I hope this passes, too. I'd hate to be around someone who gets me crying for no reason. I'm beginning to feel like I'm always crying about the stupidest things of late." He said that she wasn't that bad. "I'm sorry, did you just tell me that I'm touchy about shit?"

"No. Never that." He decided to change the subject to something less intense. "Did I tell you that Wylie put an offer in on a house? He's renting a condo now. He felt that he was putting us out by living here with us. I can't say that I blame him. It was nice having them all here, but it was a bit much with you having trouble being around them all the time." She glared at him. "I'm going to keep my mouth shut from now on. At least until the baby is born and is in college."

"They'll leave us someday." He held her until

she stopped crying. Every little thing would set her off, and he wondered if that was normal. Not that he'd ask her, but he did worry about her feelings. "Oh, Kinsey, what am I going to do with myself until the baby is born? I'm going to be dehydrated from crying so much, and you'll leave me because I can't seem to stop crying all the time. You should run for the hills before it's too late."

"It's already too late. I'm too much in love with you to ever leave you." She cried a bit more, but they were tears of happiness instead of her thinking about their unborn child leaving them someday. "How about we go out and see a movie? It might be nice to get out of the house for a couple of hours. I know that you're still working, but we can do something fun for a change."

"I'd like that." She stood up, and he pulled her into his arms again. "I'm sorry that I'm so touchy about everything. Hopefully this will pass too, and I'll be back to my old self again."

"I think any day now you're going to look back on this and wonder what all the fuss was about." She didn't look ready to cry after he told her that, and was happy. He had to be on his toes with her heart being so tender. He thought maybe if she were to tell the family about the baby, they'd be less stressed around her. With her crying about everything, they were avoiding her. He knew she didn't like that either. "There's a new comedy out, and that might be just what we need to get out of the house about. Also, before I forget again, David and Alice have invited us over for dinner on Friday night. I told them I'd have to ask you. It might be the perfect time to let them know about the baby."

"I think you might be right. I was with Alice the other day, and she kept asking me if I was all right. I think she thinks I'm dying or something along those lines. I felt bad that I couldn't tell her anything." He said that he felt the same way about David when he was around. "Did I tell you that they're about moved into their new home? They just need to hire new staff who didn't go with them."

"I'm glad that most of the staff decided to stay with us. It sure does make it easier on us when we're both working so much. How much longer do you think you'll be training your replacement? I'm betting that he's getting it all down pat, verily easily as he's been working for you for a while now." She said that she was going to be letting him run the place next week, with her there, then she was finished, but for corporate outings. "Yes, you said that he wanted nothing to do with that part of the job. It might be nice to get out and about all dressed up once in a while."

"I'd like to keep my hand in things, and that seems like the best way to do it. I'll still go into the office once a week, but that won't be full-time, and I'm looking forward to that. I just want to stay at home and make babies with you. So long as I'm not sick all the time like I am with this one. Perhaps it's because it's a girl. I hope so."

Secretly, he hoped for a little girl himself. He'd been around males all his life and wanted a little girl to hold his hand. It would be wonderful to have a son too, but he didn't care so long as they were healthy. He would be thrilled with one of each, but they'd not gotten that far yet. He just wanted her to get through this one. It was taking its toll on all of them, and they didn't even know that he was going to be a father yet.

Father. He couldn't wait to be called dad. Or whatever version that the baby came up with. He'd be happy with Dad most of all, but he wouldn't say anything. He'd never had a good role model for a parent and was thinking that he'd love it just to be able to do the things for his child that his own parents hadn't done for him. His mother had been all right, but the older he got, the more he realized that she was just as bad as their father. She could have left him at any point, and that would have made their lives so much better. Instead, she stayed with him until he killed her, and that put him in prison for the rest of his natural life.

They were headed out the door when he heard from Wylie. He knew that he'd been seeing Rosie

Donaldson, but he didn't know that it had become serious until he said that the two of them had bought a house. He nearly missed the entire conversation in thinking that his little brother might be getting married soon.

"It's a nice house, and we got it for twenty percent less than they were asking. I think that it needs very little work, but we're going to have the kitchen updated while we're waiting for them to move out. Apparently, they never use the kitchen and didn't think about it needing new appliances and new countertops." He asked for the address and told him he knew where that was. "I thought you might. It's not too far from you, about twenty minutes, but it's got a nice inground pool that we're both going to love, and there is plenty enough room in the dining room for us all to have a meal in. You should see the living room. It's going to be perfect when football season rolls around. And I have a renter for the other house I bought. The rent from it will cover the cost of the house payment as well as some of the house payments we're going to have with the new house. I think I'm going to love being a landlord if it's this easy."

"Don't count on it. I've heard of horror stories, the same as you have." He laughingly told him thanks for bursting his bubble. "I'm sorry. But you know how people are. I hope you're a better landlord than some

I've heard of, too. What am I saying? Of course, you'll be great. You're a Pennington."

"Thanks, I needed that." They were in the car when he rang off with his brother. They were headed to get something to eat at a fast-food place, then the movies.

Kinsey hadn't been to the movies in so long that he was shocked by the prices. But he kept his voice down when Meggie started to fuss at him. He just thought that twenty bucks to see a movie for two people was a great deal to pay. Then there was the bucket of popcorn that they were going to share, as well as two drinks. However, he did remember to say no ice, or he'd have nothing but ice after a couple of sips. But he paid it and kept his mouth shut. It was that or make Meggie upset with him, and he certainly didn't want that.

The movie had been all right. It had shown all the funny parts in the commercials, but he was fine with that. They'd had a good time, and he was happy that they'd gone out. Tossing away the popcorn container, he was happy to see that it didn't make Meggie's belly upset. Perhaps it was the saltiness of it, rather than it just being popcorn. Whatever it was, he didn't care. He was just happy to be out with the woman that he loved.

As they were headed home, Meggie asked for a malt, and he was more than happy to get it for her. He got one for himself, too, and was glad that they could share this one thing before going home. He thought that he was becoming sappy, but found that he didn't care. He was about as happy as he'd ever been in his life and didn't care who knew it.

He loved living in their home. He would forever be grateful to David for giving it to them when he and Meggie first started to be in love. The doctor told him right after his accident that he'd have trouble with his ankle for the rest of his life. If they were looking for a home, they'd be better off buying one that was all on one floor. They'd had that with the Winchester home, and he believed that it was fate that put David in their lives.

He'd treated them all as his sons. Kinsey himself looked up to him and asked him questions about things that he knew a son would ask a father. And just after the accident, David had stayed with him at the hospital day and night to make sure that he was all right. It was good to have a father figure around when his own father had been the worst sort of man.

After their father had killed their mother, strangling her to death after beating her, he'd made him and his brothers help try to cut her up into smaller pieces with a chainsaw while they held down the body. For years afterwards, he'd had nightmares, and on occasion since he'd grown up, he'd have them still. It had been horrific to be holding down the body of their mother while their father had tried to get the chainsaw started to do that. That was one thing that he'd never forgive him for was trying to get them to help with the demise of their mother's body when the police were on their way.

He was sure that the younger ones remembered that, even if they didn't remember their mother. The police had come to the house on a domestic call and had walked in on a bloodbath. Their father got life without parole and was currently on his twelfth year of serving that sentence. None of them had ever gone to see him since he'd been put away, and he doubted they ever would. Once, after the sale of the farm, he'd called them, but they'd made it perfectly clear that they were never going to go and see him while in prison, and he could rot there for all they cared. He was glad that he was out of their lives. It certainly made it much easier to be a wealthy man without him trying to gamble away all their wealth.

~*~

Rosie had to keep telling herself today that she loved her job. She didn't. Not today, but she was working on it. It was one of those days that you wished you'd stayed in bed and not even pulled the covers off your head. She thought that if one more thing happened, she was going to do just that and take her sorry butt home and get back in bed. It was warmer there anyway, with Wylie sleeping when she left.

He'd been staying up late working on investments. He seemed to be having a good time figuring things out, and she was proud of him. When it came to making them money, he said that so far he'd only made one mistake and he was all right with that. The return on the rest of his money was paying well, and he was finally getting the hang of what he was doing. Wylie hoped so anyway.

The two of them had been looking at furniture for their new home. All they'd found so far were the couches that they wanted for the living room and a big, screened television. He said it was for his brothers' entertainment, but she knew better. He wanted it so that he could enjoy the games on his own. Rosie was fine with that so long as he was happy. Because if he was, she was as well.

Wylie had also found a place where he could order a custom bed. It was going to be expensive, but it would fit the two of them perfectly when they were sleeping or making love. She couldn't wait to see it. It was going to be epic to sleep in something so large, and she was looking forward to it. No more falling out of bed when they moved around was going to be fun, too.

The kitchen was being done by a professional

cook. They had already decided to have a cook in the house, so having the kitchen done right the first time was going to be good. They were also getting new countertops to go with the new island in the middle of the room. The last people who had lived in the house had left the little table and chairs set for them, and she was happy. They could have breakfast or any meal at it and not be in the way of the cook and staff they were going to have.

"Chief, there's trouble down at the school. There are some older kids around pestering the younger ones that have been playing down there since school's been out." She asked if there were any adults around. "I only saw about two of them around when I drove by. The kids didn't seem to be upset or anything, but I thought I'd drive by again and see what's happening."

"All right. Just make sure that you give them the same talk as before. They're too old to be playing on the grounds when school is out. Also, make sure that little ones have adults around. They're supposed to do that too, but I've noticed that they don't seem to be around as much as I'd like. The place is too dangerous as it is without supervision. When you get older kids down there trying to 'play' with them, it gets out of hand."

"I'll take care of it now. School starts up in about a month, so we shouldn't have any trouble with them anymore after that. I think the bigger kids get bored and try to irritate the younger ones to get them going." She told him to be careful. "I will. I'll make sure they're out of there, too, before I leave. My daughter and wife go up there, and she gets annoyed when the older kids start taking the swings from the kids."

"I would too, I think." After he left, she began looking at the paperwork that had been on her desk when she came in this morning. It seemed like overnight, they could pile her desk up with more paperwork than she'd see all day when she was in the office. Most of it was petty stuff; someone dropped a candy wrapper and did not pick it up. They didn't write tickets for things like that, but they did make a note on a record in the event that it happened again. She wished they'd all stop doing the warnings and focus on the things that were important. There weren't much in the way of important things going on in this town, day or night, but she just wanted to have a clean desk when she came to work in the morning.

It took her nearly until noon to get the files put away. She never tossed out what they did, but she didn't file it either. Usually, there was no name associated with it, so it would go in a dead file anyway, but she kept them because they did, and that was what a good chief did. However, this chief was beginning to see that the job wasn't so much as being chief as being a babysitter for the town.

When her cell phone rang, she smiled. It would only be one other person besides her parents, and she was glad that he'd gotten up to talk to her. Wylie was the highlight of the day, and she would never turn down a call from him.

"I'm bringing you in lunch. I hope you've not eaten." She told him she'd been busy all morning and hadn't thought of it. "Good. I've been hungry for a big meatball sub since you mentioned it last night, and I've picked up one for each of us." She moaned. "I'm glad that you make those little noises all the time. You have no idea what they do to me."

"You showed me last night and again this morning." They both laughed. They'd been making love at the condo without too much trouble with the bed, and she loved it. "I have to get some things at the store on the way home. If you want to get them, that will save me from being late coming home."

"I can do that. I have a list of my own. They're probably the same things, so we'll compare before I head there. What did you want to drink? I brought bottled water, but I can get you a soda if you want it." She said that water was great, and he laughed. "I thought you'd say that. I also picked up some fries to go with it, so remember to share with me."

"This is going to be a big meal. Maybe we won't want any supper again until late." He said that he'd eat a salad later with her, and he said he was nearly there. Putting her phone away, she thought of what they'd done last night. They'd eaten at eleven-thirty because as soon as she got home, he attacked her at the door and they ended up in bed again. Not that she minded all that much, he made her come so many times that she was worn out all the time, but she didn't care about eating that late. It did weird things to her belly.

While she worked on clearing off her desk so that they could eat there, she thought of all the things that had happened since she met him. She'd fallen in love, bought a house with him, and now had someone in her life who was taking good care of her. She wondered what she'd do if he were to change his mind about loving her forever. Rosie didn't know what she'd do if that happened and didn't want to think about it.

"Hello, love." The kiss to her mouth was quick and nice. He started separating out the bags of food before he sat down. There seemed to be an endless supply of things coming from them, and she wondered if he had brought out the store when he'd gone shopping for water. There were even small containers of ice cream with plastic spoons and small tubs of salad. He must have been thinking he was feeding an army, and asked him about it. "You're wearing me out. And giving me a hardy appetite. I'm burning a lot of calories all the time being with you." Another kiss to her mouth, and she pulled out her sub.

"You're wearing me out too, and I have to work the next day." He told her that she should give her notice again. "I'm not ready to do that yet. I have to work, and I know how to do this job well enough that they keep me around. I'll quit sometime, but not just yet."

"I've been playing with the numbers again and doing well. I seem to have a knack for it." She told him not to get too cocky. "I'm not, trust me. I'm terrified of losing everything again, and I don't want that for us. I'm playing with little investments. It's easier to do at night when there aren't as many people around. I'm going to have to get on a daytime schedule soon, however. I miss you in the middle of the night.

She couldn't believe it when she ate most of her sub and some of the fries. She'd not realized that she was that hungry until she started eating. Wylie, of course, finished off his own and what was left of hers, plus all the French fries. She was having her ice cream when he brought up the house.

"They said they'd be out in a week. I guess they decided to have a moving company come in and take over for them. We don't have much, but I'm thinking that's what we need to do as well. I don't want to have to lift furniture all day and try to get it arranged in the house, too. Most everything that I have has been in boxes since I moved into the place I'm renting. We're renting. I don't have much at all, but a few books and my bed, and dresser. I'm looking forward to sharing it all with you."

"I have stuff at the house that I'm renting, too. Not much, either, but enough that I don't want to have to mess with it. I think getting movers will be nice, just so we're not too worn out to do anything but move it around when it gets there." He thought that was an excellent idea. "I have some clothes too, but not all that much. I usually wear sweats when I'm home, and I have several uniforms so that I don't have to do laundry every day. I'm happy for that."

After they finished their lunch with very little left over, Wylie cleaned up the mess they'd made and even took the trash out. She was thinking of putting her head back and taking a nap, but she knew that wouldn't go over well. She had a department to run, and even though very little was going on at the moment, she knew that she had to keep on top of things so that nothing got out of hand.

When Wylie left her after kissing her again, she set to work. She had plenty to do to keep her mind going, but very little of it needed her full focus. She found herself drifting off, sometimes thinking about how her life had changed since Wylie had come into her life for good. She was about as happy as she'd ever been in her life and was waiting for something to happen that would fuck it all up. Usually not so down on life, she was worried that it would happen and she'd be left alone. She didn't think that she'd ever get over losing Wylie. He'd been a part of her life since she'd been a kid and couldn't imagine a life without him in it.

Depressing herself into sadness like she hadn't had in a while, she decided to go home early and spend some time with Wylie. She hated to be like this, but things had been going so well between them that she was afraid to get too comfortable with life before it was taken away from her. She was just putting things in her locked drawer when she decided that she wasn't going to think about him leaving her anymore and focus on what they had going on now. She couldn't believe how sad she was about something that might never happen.

On her way home, she called Wylie and told him she was coming home. He was so excited to see her again that he had her sobbing. She told him that she didn't know what was wrong with her.

"You're exhausted all the time because of me. I vow not to make love to you so much." That had her burst out laughing, and she was happy that he'd been able to make her laugh. "There's my girl. We'll just have to make sure that we get enough sleep from now on. I find myself a little down in the dumps as well. I'm finding myself taking little naps during the day just to keep up with you. You're wearing me out."

"I'm sorry that you find me so irresistible. I find that I'm exhausted all the time, even when I get about eight hours of sleep. I might need to take a vacation so that I can catch up on my rest." He said that they could get married in the morning, then go on a honeymoon for a few days without sex. They could go anywhere she wanted. "To bed at home. Just get enough sleep so that I'm not chasing my tail all the time with sleep."

"Perfect. We need to find us a better way to be together, too. I mean, having meals together. I missed having supper with you because we're getting it so late. And like you said, it messes with my belly too to be eating too late." They talked about her vacation, and she would just have to put in for it. She had a lot of time built up because she rarely, if ever, took any time off. "I've never had a job where I had a vacation coming to me. I worked for the family farm for all my life, so I didn't have any time for myself, much less for a vacation. I'm looking forward to having some time with you all to myself."

By the time she got home, they had it all planned out. They were going to take a couple of days to hang around the house, then go to the Smokies. Neither one of them had been there, and she was looking forward to it as much as he was. As soon as she was in the door, they started making plans. She called the mayor and let him know that she was taking some much-needed time off. He agreed to give her two weeks that she requested, and they were off and running. It was going to be fun to be able to not have to answer to anyone but themselves. She thought that she was looking forward to that as much as she was to being able to sleep in.

Chapter 5

The vacation they took was better than either of them had dreamed of it being. He was glad to be home, but he'd go back anytime he had some time off. It had been all the time that they got to spend together that had been the best part. Since they didn't know anyone around them, it was nice to be able to spend some much-needed time with just the two of them. Neither one of them seemed to be as stressed when they got back, either. And they were able to move into the house earlier than they'd expected to.

They had a few days left on their vacation, so he set it up so that the movers could get both places lined up to be packed up on the same day. They just wanted to move in at this point, and Wylie was happy that he had the resources to get it done. He'd hate to think of all this doing it on his own.

Wylie was glad for the vacation they'd been on for two reasons. It had been nice to get away, but he also got to know more about Rosie. They'd spent their entire lives together and knew so very little about each other. She was well rested, too, and for that, he was happy.

"I'm thinking that we need to make sure we get away like this once a year, if not more." He said he was all for that. Even if they stayed at home. "Yes, I was going to say that too. It was nice of your brothers to cover for you while we were gone, and I'd do the same for them. It was just too much fun not to be able to look forward to something like that once in a while."

"I agree. Also, when we have kids, we'll have to take them with us. Even, like you said, even if it's only to have a nice vacation at home." Nodding at him, she closed her eyes and leaned back on the new couch that had only just arrived. "We'll have to make sure we get enough of the other things we need, too. Lamps in here would be a good thing."

"I was thinking of how nice it was that it's dark. But I suppose you're right. We do need some lighting." She snuggled down on the couch, and he watched her. In less than ten minutes, he knew she'd be asleep, and he had figured out that was one of his favorite pastimes, just watching her sleep for a few minutes. "I can't believe that I need a nap right now. I slept most of the way home, and now here I am resting again. Just a few minutes and I'll be fine and ready to go."

He knew that about her, too. That after about ten minutes of her laying there with her eyes closed, she'd be awake and energized again. He envied that about her. A power nap could do for her what he'd not been able to do for himself. Get rested enough to go on with their day. He knew it was because he'd been watching her every move. He found it mesmerizing to know every little thing about her, including her sleeping habits.

Getting up when she snored softly, he made his way to the kitchen to see what he could get them in the way for dinner. They had a cook starting on Monday, so for now it was just the two of them. Kinsey had given them some beef that he had left over from when they were living on the ranch, so he put on one of the roasts so that they could have it for dinner. He was pretty good at cooking, but he didn't want to do it all the time any more than she did.

After getting the roast on and the kitchen cleaned up, he made his way to the office he'd taken after checking up on Rosie. She was still sleeping, so he left her alone. After getting his computer set up the way that he wanted — they were still getting things put where they wanted them — he pulled up the investment portfolio that he'd been using since he'd been doing his own investments. He knew that Bodi and Ara had hired someone to do their investments, and he was thinking of going that route as well. Meggie said that she could use their firm that did it for her and Kinsey. He might do that and go with someone whom he could trust. He didn't want to run out of money because he didn't know what he was doing.

"You let me sleep too much." He moved back from the desk so that she could sit on his lap. "I had the strangest dream. I dreamt that I'd met the man of my dreams, and he was you. What a strange dream, don't you think?" She laughed when he did.

"I'm thinking of finding someone else to do our investments." He told her what he'd been able to figure out. "I'm having fun with them, but I'm not all that good at it yet, and I don't want us to run out of money too soon. I figure that someday we'll be able to look back on this and wonder what all the fuss was about, but for now, I'm not sure what I'm doing. I don't want to mess up."

"I understand. It's difficult to start a new project when you don't have all the information. I would imagine that it might take a person years to learn the job." He agreed with her. "I'm going to have to get things rolling on my job. I've become too pampered with being at home, and now I find that I don't want to go back. I will, even if it's only for a short while, but I'm enjoying only thinking about work once in a while instead of all the time like I was. This break showed me too that I'm not needed all that much now, and I think, while a little bit sad, I can take the time off without hurting the department."

"I know what you mean. It's like life went on

without us stressing about it, and now that we've come back to the real world, it's kind of sad that barely anyone missed us." She laughed and stood up. "Are you leaving me? I thought we'd use the top of my desk for a little fun. What do you say?"

"I have to decline. I've started my period, and I have cramps really bad." He said he was sorry and asked if there was anything that he could do for her. "Nothing. I'm all right. I think that's why I took such a long nap. My body is dealing with too much today."

After she left him, he decided to make the calls about their investments. He'd been putting it off in favor of just doing it himself, but he again didn't want to mess with their money too much. As soon as he was off the phone with the guy that Meggie told him about, he felt better about it. Like Rosie had said, it was better to leave that sort of work to the professionals so that they had money when he needed it.

He was sure that he was so worried about money because of the way they'd grown up. They'd been so poor all the time that they were one breakdown from a disaster. They had a lot of help from their neighbors, but their own equipment was old and wearing out, and they could barely afford to feed themselves at times, not to mention the cattle and chickens that were depending on them. It had been a scary time growing up without. But their grannie had made sure that there was meat on the table even if there was nothing else. She'd been good to them and for them.

She'd told Kinsey to sell the land to the highest bidder, and that's what he'd done. Splitting the money six ways evenly so that they could all reap from the land. David Winchester had purchased all the land from them and made them all millionaires. The man himself was a billionaire, and he was happy to know him. He'd been like a father figure to them all since he'd met them.

Making several more calls, he was ready to call it a day when his phone rang. He would usually let it go to voicemail, but since he'd made so many calls today, he thought that he'd better answer it. He couldn't believe it was the prison where his father was. They were asking him if he was Kinsey Pennington.

"I'm not, but I'm one of his brothers. What's going on that has you calling here? I know for a fact that we said that we didn't want to hear from him again." The man said his name was Warden Jefferson, and he was calling to tell him that their father was dead. "What happened to him?"

"He got into a fight over potato chips of all things, and the other man broke his neck for trying to steal them. It was over almost as soon as it started, as your father didn't have a chance. We didn't see it happen, but it's on CCTV here at the prison if you were to ever want to look at it. I'm sorry for your loss." He didn't know what to say, so he said nothing. If he was honest with himself, he was happy that he was gone. It had been his biggest fear that he'd get out somehow and terrorize them. "Would anyone from your family like to claim his body? I know for a while there he was talking to one of you, so I was wondering if you've had a change of heart about him."

"No, we only spoke with him the one time, and that was it. That's all it took for us to tell him not to call here anymore." He said he was sorry. "I am as well, but not like you think. Thanks for telling me, and I'll make sure to pass it along to the others. You can bury him out there in the unmarked graves as far as we're concerned."

He did wonder if he should have asked his brothers about their father, but he was sure that they were under the same opinion he was about him. He was gone and good riddens. As soon as he got off the phone, he called Kinsey. He was the oldest and would know more than they did about what was going on about them being called.

"Good." He told him that was pretty much what he'd said about him. "I've been wondering if he'd be buried up there or not. I'm glad that we no longer have to worry about him getting out anytime too soon. I know that was in the back of my mind a great deal.

Or when I ever thought about him. Which I tried not to do."

"I guess we should tell the others. I don't know that they'll care anymore than we do. But they should know." He asked his big brother if he'd been talking to him. He said he'd not. "I didn't either. I wanted nothing to do with him after we had that talk with him after our accident. It was bad enough that he figured out that we were still around. Having him call us just after you and me had that accident really put me off. He never did ask how we'd been feeling. I think that stuck with me more than anything he said to us."

"He was a selfish bastard, and I'm glad that he's gone. I don't plan on telling my kids he was around either. I'm just going to say that he's dead and that will be the end of it." Wylie said that he hoped it would be that easy. "I do as well. But my luck, they'll want to know all about him, and I'll tell them if they ask. But as far as I'm concerned, he was dead to me the moment he tried to start that chainsaw."

"I have dreams about that still. Do you?" He said that he'd think about it, but nothing bothered him at night. "I'm glad to hear that. I know that Ara still has some nightmares about him. He was the youngest and may never get over that part."

"I don't think any of us will." There was that, and Wylie knew that to be true. "What else did he say?

Anything about us picking up his body? I'm not going to bury him next to Mom if we have to."

"I told him to bury him in their fields for all I cared. We wouldn't be claiming the body no matter what. I didn't ask, and probably should have, whether they would be sending us the things that he left behind. I don't want those either. I should have thought to ask." Kinsey said if they arrived for any of them, he'd make sure to burn them. There was nothing this man had that would have made them want to see what he'd left them. "We can have a ceremony about them and burn them in the trash pile in the back of my property. Since we had the house done, we have accumulated a great deal of crap."

"Good. If it comes to that, we'll take care of them that way. Otherwise, we just go on with our lives and pretend that he didn't matter to us one bit." He said that he didn't. "Nope, not at all. Especially not enough for us to get worked up over about it."

After asking Kinsey to help him make the calls, they were finished in no time. His brothers that he called, didn't want to have anything to do with his remains either, and he was glad for that. Telling them that they were going to have a celebration if the prison was to send them his things, they all thought that was the way to go. It was sad to him that a man had had six sons, and they wanted nothing to do with him in either life or death. He supposed that it was his own fault. As he'd made his bed and now must lie in it.

He never hated the man so much as he did that day. It hadn't been a day that started out like something terrible was going to happen. Mom and the rest of them had been making strawberry jelly when he'd come home and demanded that she let him have a party for his drinking buddies. When she'd said no, he beat her nearly to death, then strangled her for good measure. There had been jam everywhere mixed with the blood, and to this day, he couldn't eat any kind of jam without thinking about that day. He thought his brothers did the same thing and never touched the stuff again.

~*~

Gleason decided that he was going to build. He knew that it would take longer for him to get into a real house, but he was sick of looking at other people's houses and wanted one of his own. He thought for sure that Wylie and Kinsey got the last two good houses around town. They'd been looking for one since he'd started and didn't like what he was seeing. He found a blueprint for one that he'd like about five years ago and hoped that he could still get them to have his own home. He knew nothing about building something other than what he'd been able to find on the internet. It sounded complicated yet easy, and that's what he was going to do.

"You said you have the land picked out? He said that it was some of the land that they'd not been able to buy back from the neighborhood lands. "I'll make sure that it's available. You never know after all this time if it's still a good piece of land."

Howard the banker had been a friend of the family since before he'd been born. It was mostly his grannie who had dealt with him, and he was glad that she had a good relationship with the banker. It made things easier for him when he wanted to talk to him about banking needs. He'd also been investing in things online that he knew would benefit the town and was glad that he'd had that as well.

It took him most of the day to find someone who could build his home. He finally ended up talking to David about his builder and went with him. He seemed not to have any complaints about him, and that was as good a recommendation as it came. Getting it started now would mean that he might be in it by next spring. He wasn't going to hire extra men to get it done sooner, as David did. David was a billionaire, and that was all on him.

He was still living with Kinsey and Meggie. The others had moved out on their own, and he was happy for them. The three of them got along well, and he was glad for the company sometimes. He was getting bored by not working as much as he had before, and that worried him a little. Boredom usually led to trouble, and he didn't want to be caught not doing something when he had plenty of time to work. He decided that was the next thing on his list of stuff to do. Get a job.

He didn't want to farm anymore. He'd had enough of that working for himself. But he did want to do something, even if it only got him out of the house for a couple of hours a day. He knew what he had planned for next spring season, and that was to till up gardens with old Tim. He didn't know who had named the tractor, but he was glad that he was still working for him.

Gleason was just thinking about getting something to eat when he saw his brothers, Ara and Raphael. They, too, were going to get something to eat at the little diner and asked if he could join them. They were expecting Bodi to join them, but he was running late and told them to start without him. He ordered himself two double cheeseburgers with fries, while the other two ordered a pizza to share. He didn't know how well that was going to go over; they didn't share well, but he was staying out of it if they got into a fight. He wanted a meal, and if he had to put up with them to do it, he was all right with that.

The food was being set in front of them when Bodi joined them. He asked if he would give him one of his burgers when it came. Knowing that he could always get him something else to eat if he didn't want to give up one of his meals, he handed him one of the burgers while he ate his.

"Did you hear that there's going to be a big to-do in the town over? They're having a street fair and everything in a few weeks. Something about their homecoming. We all know that when Dresden has their homecoming, it rains for four straight days. I hope they have better luck than we do." They talked about Frazeysburg having their homecoming as well. "I wonder what they have a homecoming for. I didn't think that anyone left this town once they were born here. We certainly didn't."

"No, and I don't plan on it either. I love this little town." They all agreed, and when Bodi's plate came with his cheeseburgers, he gave him his second one like he said. "Where else can you get a burger this great and not have to spend a large amount of money? Nowhere unless you go to that fancy shop in downtown Zanesville. Eighteen dollars for a single burger without any fries or milkshake is a lot of money to put out."

"You're just mad because she charged you full price when you asked her out. Flirting doesn't always get you what you want, you know?" They teased Bodi for a while, then they ate the rest of their dinner. "I'm going to have to get me someone to cook for me when I move out. I've been living with Kinsey and Meggie, and they have a cook. I've gotten used to it, and I love being able to have a full meal and not have to clean up after myself." He was eating the last of his fries when he told them about the house he was going to have built.

"Will you stay with Kinsey? I'm sure with the baby coming along, it'll be odd there. Kinsey is already showing signs of being stressed out." He said he'd stay until he couldn't anymore. "That's a good plan. Just don't hurt Meggie's feelings. I know with the baby coming along, that's what made her so tender but I hate that she cries at the least bit of commotion."

"You should see Kinsey when he makes her cry. All he has to do is mention that she's doing something wonderful, and he gets all stressed up. Like her crying is a part of him or something. I'm betting by the time the baby's here, things will even out. She's just tender like that because her body is working hard on creating a life." He was asked how he was so knowledgeable all of a sudden. "When she started crying about everything, even before they told us, I knew something was wrong. So I looked it up on the computer and found out she was more than likely going to have a baby, and I just kept reading from there."

"Why didn't you tell us?" He said he might

have been wrong. "Yeah, okay, I can see that. Better to keep your mouth shut than to ruin their surprise. I was, too. I know most of us were."

"I think they told David and Alice before us. I think they were hoping that he'd stop pushing for a large wedding. He wants to show off his kids. He thinks of all of us like his kids now that we've been hanging out with them." Gleason agreed and said he thought of him as a father figure and went to him when he had questions. "I do too. Even going to Alice sometimes when I have questions. She's pretty good at not laughing at me when I do have something to find out."

The four of them finished up their meals and sat and talked for a while. There were no others in the diner, so they didn't feel bad about taking up the table. They did pay their checks so that the waitress wouldn't be worried. He might well have too, but for the fact that they all had money now when they hadn't before.

When they got on the subject of living in town again, he tuned them out. They'd been going over the same thing since they'd sold the farm, and he didn't understand what they were upset about. Kinsey said he didn't want any of their money, and that was final. He too wanted to give his brother extra money for helping them out with sharing the money, but he wasn't going to take it, so he moved on. Then they started talking about the new building that was being added to the high school because of the taxes paid on the land that David bought.

"I also heard that the football team is getting all new uniforms, too. Along with the band. They've had the same uniforms since I went to school there, and that's been a long time." They figured up how long it had been and were all shocked that they'd been out of high school that long. "I guess we're older than I thought. I have to get going with my house so that I'm not too old to enjoy it. I keep thinking about what Grannie said to us about living on the land that would kill us. I'm so happy that things are settled with the land. I was never so happy that Kinsey agreed to sell it when he did."

"I just love that he took a vote on it. He said it was all of us or none of us would be making out from the sale. Do you really think he would have done that had there been one of us who didn't want to leave the farm?" Bodi said he thought that Kinsey knew that everyone was going to be leaving and made it easier for the rest of us. "Do you suppose he ever regrets it? I mean, selling the farm."

"I think that he's a happy man with a wife, money, and a baby on the way. Not necessarily in that order, but you understand what I'm saying." They all agreed and decided that they were all happier, too. "I know I am. Working two jobs and trying to keep the bills up was killing us all. Even when we were thinking about the sale, I don't think that any of us believed it would sell. I know that I didn't think it would happen. Not in our lifetime. Maybe twenty years from now, perhaps, but not on the same day that it went live to sell. We have a lot to be thankful for about Meggie, too. She's the one who got all the right people together so that it would be now. She's the best wife of Kinsey there is."

They all laughed at that, and he wondered what his wife would be like if she ever came around. He wasn't really looking for anyone; hell, he didn't date all that much. But he did find his mind wandering from time to time, what it would be like to be in love with someone the way that Wylie and Kinsey were.

After their dinner, they walked around town together to see what they could get into. He enjoyed having all the free time and was glad not to be working on two farms to make ends meet. But he was going to do what he said in the spring and knew he'd enjoy doing that little bit for the people around. He might even make someone happy enough to share some of their fresh crop with him, and he'd love that as well.

After it started getting dark, they went their separate ways. He was headed back to Kinsey's house when his cell phone rang. It was Wylie. He wanted to know if he wanted to get breakfast in town in the morning, as Rosie had to work.

"I'd love that. I've missed you." They talked again about the things going on around town, and he gave him an update on the things he'd heard from his brothers. "We need to get together once a week or so that we can catch up on gossip. There is a lot of it going around, and now that we don't have to work from sunup to sundown, we can listen to what's going on."

"I've been getting some information from Rosie. If it's going on around town, she's the first person to know about it." He supposed that, as chief of police, she would hear the best gossip. "I'll make a list of things to tell you, and you can tell me what you've heard. Where do you want to meet?"

"Scotties Den, if you don't mind. I had dinner at the diner, so I'm thinking I need to change it up a bit." He told him how he'd had dinner with the others, and Wylie said he was jealous. "We're all jealous of you and Kinsey having your wives. You did get married, didn't you?"

"This morning. She had to go right back to work, too, so there was no time for us to have much of a honeymoon." Gleason laughed at his brother. "Yes, laugh it up, little brother. You'll be here in my position soon enough."

"I've been thinking about that very same thing.

I'm not saying that I'm looking for the next Mrs. Pennington, but I have given it some thought. I'm not sure that I'm ready for a wife and all that comes with it. It hit you two so quickly and hard that it's hard to imagine it doing the same thing with us. I think I'll be engaged for years before I actually get married. I don't want a whirlwind courtship while I'm building my dream house."

They talked about him building his home, and he thought that he was going in the right direction for him. Wylie had found the perfect house for them, and that was wonderful. But he wanted all new things in his place, including carpets if it came to that. Gleason said that he was going to keep himself hidden away until he was ready.

"Good luck with that. I'm sure that none of us are going to be ready when she comes along. I knew I wasn't." Gleason didn't say anything, and that seemed to be fine with his brother. "Oh well, I'll see you in the morning. I'm going to be the one with the sappy look on his face."

"Good night." After getting off the phone with his brother, he went up to his room. He knew that Meggie and Kinsey had plans tonight, as it was the cook's night off, so that was why he'd eaten at the diner. But he wasn't going to make a habit of going out. He liked being able to do it, but he had to save his money too.

Chapter 6

Wylie loved his office now that it was finished. He'd been working on it for the past three days and thought that he had it just the way he wanted it. He didn't have any work to be going on right now, but he thought that if he needed something to be looked up, he'd have the perfect place to do it in. He closed his laptop and went to find Rosie. She'd been interviewing cooks today, and he didn't envy her the job. He wouldn't know the first thing about interviewing anyone for any kind of job.

She said she'd only just hired them two cooks as they both wanted to work part-time. He asked her how that would work for them, and she smiled.

"One will work during the daytime and the other in the evening. It'll be nice this way because we can work around their schedule. And since they don't want the same day off, we can have meals every day so that we don't have to fend for ourselves. I like that best of all. It will also save us from going out so much. While I do enjoy a meal out with you, it gets too expensive to have to do every day."

"I've made arrangements for us to have a

little garden next year. I miss having fresh vegetables around all the time. It was usually the only way that we could afford to eat so well. It won't be until spring, but it'll be something to do too throughout the summer months." She asked him about pumpkins. "We usually grew those too, but the pie-eating kind. Did you want to grow pumpkins for the front of the house, too?"

"Sure. If we have any leftovers, we can give them to your brothers. I did notice that Kinsey and Meggie have a garden. She told me that David had had a garden in before they moved into the house. It's well established, too, in that they have one every year." He thought that they could do that as well. "I thought you'd say that, and I'm happy for it too. I love fresh carrots that are right out of the garden. I don't even care if they're a little dirty when I eat them."

"I'm the same way when it comes to tomatoes. I love taking a salt shaker out to the garden and pulling a nice ripe tomato off the vine and eating it with a good dose of salt. It's still warm from the sun, and the flavor is so much better than you can get in a store." He rubbed his belly. "Now that's all I want is a tomato fresh from the garden." She told him that was one of her favorite memories of growing up with her grandma. "I miss mine so much. I think of her all the time and wonder if she's looking down on us, smiling because we sold the farm. It was her fondest wish for us to sell it and become men of leisure. I loved her a great deal."

"I did mine too. She was forever there for me." She said she depended on her parents a great deal as well. "I know. I've seen the three of you together, and you make a great family picture."

For the rest of the evening, they talked about memories they had as children growing up in their homes. He didn't have all that good of memories, not of his parents, but he did remember his grandma and how she had brought them up to be good men. But she wanted more for them than working themselves to death working on the Pennington farm. With her dying breath, she told Kinsey to sell it and get on with their lives while they were still young enough to enjoy it. Not to be broken down by running a farm that would suck them dry.

When it was time for dinner, the roast was perfect. He'd even browned up some potatoes to go with it, as well as a nice fresh salad. It had tomatoes on it, but they were from the grocery store and not as good as they'd been talking about. He couldn't wait for summer to roll around again so that he could tinker with a little garden just for the two of them.

It was nearly midnight when they went to bed. Their new bed would be there tomorrow, and he was looking forward to that. It was larger than could be found on the market, and they'd have to have sheets especially made for it, but he didn't care. He was looking forward to having a bed big enough that they could sleep together and play around in it as well.

Wylie had two interviews tomorrow about part-time work. He didn't want to be working full-time just yet and was glad that they understood that. One of the interviews was working for Meggie, and he had not told her that he applied. It was going to be a good job, and he was looking forward to maybe getting it. As soon as he set his alarm, he was ready to go to sleep for about twelve hours. Or more, but knew that he had to get up sometime sooner than that.

"I'm looking into giving my notice at work too." The room was dark, and Rosie whispered in the night. "I've had enough. I've been doing this job since I got out of college, and it's too much for me right now. I love the fact that you have money so that I can take my time finding something else."

"*We* have money right now, not just me." She said that she knew that, but would forget when she was talking about it. "I don't want you to forget that we're a couple and everything that I have is yours too. I love you and want you to be happy."

"I am happy. Happier than I thought I'd ever be." She snuggled around him, and he held her. "I'm exhausted again. I think I'm going to go and see the doctor soon to see if he can give me something to keep me going. It might be something so simple as being stressed all the time, but I'm going to make an appointment in the morning. It can't hurt."

"I've been worried about you, too. You seem to doze off at the drop of a hat. While I love watching you rest, you do it a lot. And stress isn't anything to mess with. I want you to be happy and awake." She didn't say anything, and he realized that she was asleep. He was all right with it now, as it was bedtime, but he did worry about her. Perhaps when she quit her job, she'd be more rested, but he didn't know for sure. He hoped it was nothing too serious. He worried about her.

Wylie didn't fall asleep right away. He had too many things on his mind and was worried about Rosie. Getting up after he was sure that she'd not wake up, he left the room in favor of going to his office and looking at things on the internet. He didn't use his phone for fear of waking Rosie. He would just read for a little while and then go back to bed. He'd done it before, and it usually gave him a good night's sleep to be able to read for a little while.

Going back up to bed at around two, he was less stressed and feeling good about going to bed. He slipped into the bed and was happy when Rosie wrapped herself around him. It was the best part of sleeping with her. She knew how to give the best hugs in the middle of the night. He knew when he woke in the morning, he'd be refreshed and ready to go. Mornings were his favorite part of the day.

His first interview didn't go so well. The man was sort of pissed at him that he wanted to work. He said that there were people out there who needed a hand up, and he was just taking it from them. Then why did he have a help-wanted sign in his window if there were so many people who needed a job? He didn't understand people at all. As he was making his way to the other interview, he hoped that it would go better. He'd not told anyone that he was related to Meggie by marriage and hoped that it wouldn't make a difference.

The second interviewer was running behind, and Meggie found him in the waiting room, waiting for the man to get his shit together. She asked him why he hadn't said anything, and he told her that he wanted to get the job because he was qualified and not part of the family.

"I would have hired you right away. Even for all your experience in working on the farm, you'd be a good asset for us. Just as a consultation on farms that we might buy up to resell would be something that I could use you for." He told her that he didn't want her to make up a job for him. "I'm not, I promise. I really do need someone who's an expert on farms and what they might need in the way of loans. However,

I'm beginning to think that all of them need a little help now and again."

"You're right on that. We could have used more help than we asked for when I think about it. If not for Howard at the bank, there are times when I think we would have lost everything. Especially when it came to the little things like a hot water heater. I think that Kinsey nursed ours along for more than a year so that we'd be able to take a halfway hot shower. Still, that left us washing our clothing in ice-cold water, and they'd not get all that clean." She said that he'd told her about the loan that he'd gotten. "We have a lot of terrible memories of the place, but a lot of good ones too. We were all together, and that was important to us. We didn't have much, but we did have each other to lean on, and I think that's the only way that we were able to hold onto the farm."

"You're going to be perfect for the job I have in mind." He said that he had an interview with someone twenty minutes ago. "I know. Lucky for us, I was able to see you first. He might have hired you, but your talent would have been wasted on what he was going to hire you for. My way, I get the best of both worlds. You working for us and your knowledge about farms."

She took him to Human Resources for him to get his paperwork finished up to work. Since she'd done background checks on all of them when she'd helped them with the sale of the farm, it was much quicker than he thought it would have been. She was all right with him only working part-time, and she said she'd have it no other way. He had a wife to attend to, too, and she didn't want a job to interfere with that.

"I know what it's like to have someone around you that you love. I can't stand to be away from Kinsey more than a few hours, and he always makes me feel special when he's with me. Even going to a burger place after some appointment, he makes it feel like it's a five-star restaurant, no matter what we're having." He told her that he was happy for her and also said that Kinsey had been the best big brother all his life. "I love how you six hug all the time. It makes me feel like there is some goodness in the world yet. I'm hoping that the rest of your brothers find someone to love them, too. We'll be one big happy family when we're all wed and happy."

After HR, he was shown to an office he would be using. He didn't know if he needed an office, but she said that it would be good for him to have one so that he could spread out there. Also, she hinted that Rosie could come by and see him, and they'd have the privacy that they needed. He could feel his face heat up at that and loved that she was so open with it. He really did love this woman like a sister and was glad that she'd made Kinsey so happy.

"I'm going to hire you a full-time secretary so that you have someone to field calls when you're not in. I have that now, and I love it. It makes it so much easier to keep up with things and not have to be here all the time. I know that's important to you. I know that it is for me as well." He got around to asking her how she was feeling. "Much better than I was before. The doctor put me on some vitamins, and that's helped a great deal. I'm still kind of touchy, but nothing like I was before. And I've been walking on the treadmill once a day so that I can stay in shape. Nothing too hard, about three miles a day, but it's enough so that when I go to bed at night, I'm sleeping better, too. How is Rosie? I heard that she was going to quit her job soon."

"She'll be working part-time if she wants to find a job. I'm leaving that up to her." He didn't mention that she'd been going to the doctor about sleeping all the time. They would when they had an answer; they didn't have any right now. "She and I had a wonderful vacation in the Smokies. I'd recommend that to anyone who needs to get away. The phone service is terrible."

They both laughed, and she left him to go home. He was excited about having a job that paid well and that he was going to be working on something that he knew a little about. His other interview had been for working in a pizza shop, and he was glad that the man had turned him down.

~*~

Rosie couldn't believe that she was pregnant. She had asked the doctor about having her period, and he told her that sometimes that happened. After giving her a thorough checkup, he said that both she and the baby were fine, other than she needed to eat more regularly. Their meal times hadn't been set in stone yet, and she was glad that she was being made to do something about it. He told her that she just needed to nap when she was tired; it was just her body getting used to creating a life. She couldn't wait to tell Wylie about it and was glad that he was home when she got there.

"I have a job." She was so happy for him that she nearly forgot her own news. "I start when she has a farm that she's looking at. But I can go in and meet the person who works for me. Also, I need to set up my office the way that I want it. She said she'd make sure that I have a computer there when I do come in."

"That's wonderful news. I have some of my own. We're going to have a baby." He seemed to not understand at first as he went on about his job. Then he looked at her and asked her what she'd said. "I said you're going to be a daddy in about eight months."

She went on to explain to him about her period as well as why she was so exhausted all the time. After telling him about their meal times and needing them to be better scheduled, he picked her up and swung her around. She was so happy that she burst into tears.

"I'd been worried you'd not think it was a good idea right now." He said that he was thrilled beyond words. "I can tell. I'm so happy. My parents are going to be happy as well. I'm not telling them right away, but I'm going to soon. It's time we got the nursery set up for us and find us a nanny. With both of us working part-time, it'll be nice to have someone for the middle of the night, don't you think? My parents had someone when they had me."

"I think that whatever you want, I'm going to be fine with it. I can't believe that we're going to be having a baby, too. And you're right, I don't want to tell anyone right away. It'll be our secret." He put his hand on her still flat belly. "I noticed when I saw Meggie today that she's starting to show a little. I didn't say anything to her. I didn't want her to cry, but she's looking like she's glowing, too. She said that she was feeling better."

"The doctor said that I should be feeling better in a few weeks. It's just my body adjusting to having a child. I was so worried it might be something bad." He admitted to her that he'd been worried too. "I'm betting that you looked it up when you were on the internet. I try my best not to do that, but I looked too. There are all kinds of things that could be causing this, and I'm glad it's just a baby. Our baby. Just knowing that it's a baby will make me sleep better, too. And I'm supposed to take a nap when I want one. I'm glad for that too. I hated that I was missing time with you because I was so tired all the time."

"He said in a few weeks you'd feel better. I'm glad for that." He kissed her gently and told her how much he loved her. "You're the best thing that has ever happened to me, and I couldn't be happier about anything going on right now."

"Me either." They talked about the baby for a while and decided they needed to go out and celebrate. It was still early enough that their cook hadn't started anything tonight, and they were going to go to Columbus again for seafood. It was fast becoming their favorite place to eat, and he loved that they both would have such a good time, too. He couldn't wait to tell everyone as he'd been so worried, but he'd keep it to himself for as long as Rosie wanted. He couldn't believe that he was going to be a daddy soon and squeezed Rosie's hand when he got up off the floor. "I'm not a delicate flower, you know. I've been a cop for well over five years. But this makes me want to quit even more. I know this is a small town, but I'm worried about having to carry a gun all the time. I carry it for a reason, and I hate to think that something might come up that I'd have to pull it. I'm going to be more careful about wearing my vest, too."

"I'm glad to hear that. I don't want you to take any chances either. You have to be there for us, or I don't know what I'd do without you around. I'm glad that you're quitting now. I'll feel so much better when your notice is up." She said she might have to work until they found someone to replace her. "So long as they're looking and not treating you the way that they were Bodi about finding a replacement. I will worry about you until you get home every night more than ever before. You're my everything."

"I love you too." They were going to have a baby; his mind kept rolling that around in his head. He was going to be the best father that he knew how to be and was looking forward to getting advice from David. He didn't have any kids, but he'd been a great dad to them, and he was sure he'd have some good advice.

Wylie got dressed up to go into town. He'd even been able to convince Rosie not to wear heels. They hurt her feet, and there was no point in being uncomfortable at this point in her life. Plus, her feet were a little swollen from walking around all day in dress shoes. He even brought her slippers with them so that she could put them on after they ate. He was going to go overboard in pampering his little momma until she had enough. Wylie didn't think that would take all that long for her to be thumping him on the back of the head because she'd had enough.

Dinner was spectacular. He'd gotten the crab legs again, and Rosie had gotten herself some crab cakes. He loved them too and was glad that she was willing to share with him. He did the same with his legs. After dinner, they both got dessert of ice cream and pie, and were headed home when she took another nap. He thought that she was adorable in her nice dress and fuzzy slippers.

Getting her home, she said she was ready for bed. He expected no less than that from her. As soon as she was in bed, she fell asleep with a smile on her face. Getting in bed with her, suddenly tired himself, he held her tightly to his body and marveled that she was carrying his child, and he could hardly contain himself.

Wylie vowed to be the best father he could be and do for his child all the things that his dad had never done for him. He only wished the one time that his mother could have been around, but she wouldn't have been too happy. She'd always told them that she didn't want to be a grandma ever, and that was the end of it. He couldn't understand why someone wouldn't want to see their children have their own family. Wylie thought that it would be the best thing in the world to see their children having little ones about.

Going to sleep, he was nearly there when he

thought of something else. They'd have to get the nursery ready now so that it would be ready when they needed it. It was just off the master suite, and he'd never done anything to it other than to have it painted before they moved in. He'd actually been thinking of changing it to a media room for the two of them so they could have their bed close when it was bedtime. He had plenty of time, he thought to himself. Just about eight months to get it ready.

Drifting off to sleep, he couldn't keep himself from smiling all the time. He was giddy about being a father and was having a hard time sleeping when he wanted to get up and shout out to the world what was going on. Holding Rosie tighter, he finally felt himself falling asleep.

Waking in the middle of the night when there was a cold spot next to him on the bed, he sat up looking for Rosie. She said that she'd had to use the bathroom and that was all. If he was going to be this worried about her in the middle of the night, he was never going to survive her going to work every day. Deciding that he was just going to have to, he decided to make sure that she knew he loved her every time she left the house.

When she got back into bed, he held her. She was chilled and shaking a bit, so he rubbed her arms with his hands to warm her up. As soon as she fell asleep again, he knew that he was going to be up for a while and got up to go to the office. If he kept this up, he was going to have to get himself a closer office. Or maybe he'd just stop getting up in the middle of the night so that he could sleep better. Laughing to himself, he was in his office in no time, looking up how far along Rosie would be by her due date, and was thrilled there was so much information on the internet that he could find.

By one thirty, he'd had enough and made his way to bed. He had a better understanding of the things that Rosie was going through and was happy for that. He was happy that he'd not found much in the way of bad news when he'd been looking things up and was satisfied when he got into bed. Falling asleep right away felt good, and he was going to sleep better because he had a bit more information.

Waking before his alarm went off, he was happy to see that Rosie was already up. She'd been sleeping in most mornings, and he'd have to call her several times to get her going in the morning for work. When she got out of the shower, she looked like she was rested, and he told her so.

"Just knowing that there isnt anything wrong with me makes me feel so much better. I wasn't going to admit this to anyone, but I was afraid of what the doctor might have found. You can imagine my surprise when he found a baby." She hugged him as she got ready for work. "I've decided to give my notice today. I've got a rough draft of my resignation in my head right now, and I think it'll be all right. I'm not mentioning the baby, but I am saying that I have other obligations that are keeping me from doing my job as well as I wish I could. I think it'll be something the mayor will be all right with. As I said, I might have to work a little bit more until he finds me a replacement, but I won't know until I talk to him."

"I hope he tells you that he's been looking all along since you got married. That would be something if he had someone in mind already." She said she'd not count on that. "No, I won't. I was just doing some wishful thinking out loud."

After she left for work, running slightly behind because he wanted to hold her, he got himself ready to go to his new work. He had to order supplies, not having any idea what that might entail, but he was going to set up his computer and desk so that when he needed it, it would be ready for him. He didn't see her needing him all that much and figured that in a few months, she'd decide that it wasn't worth having him on her payroll, so he'd take it while he had it. He did find him a map to hang up of the area so that he could be prepared for something local that might go on. It was noon when Rosie called him.

"The mayor said he was going to miss me but

understood. He said that he'd put it out there that he needed a new police chief today and see how soon he could get someone to take over. I told him that I'd work until he did, and he was pleased with that." She mentioned that she had some more vacation time that he was going to allow her to turn in for hours so that she could use them up. "That'll be an extra paycheck that I wasn't expecting, so we can put it toward the nursery. I don't want to start on that right away because of the horror stories I heard from people who would lose their baby early on. I'm not too worried about that. I feel great, other than being tired all the time, and I want to be healthy when the baby arrives. You understand, don't you?"

"I do. I have to tell you that I was thinking the same thing. That we'd get the nursery ready now so we'd not have to do it at the last minute. But I like your way much better. It gives us a chance to see what sort of things we're going to need and want. I want it all, but I've read there is no reason for buying some of the things they advertise for babies. We'll just have to do our research on them." She agreed and told him that she had to do. "I do as well. I'm getting my office set up the way that I want. I love you, Rosie Pennington."

"And I love you, Wylie Pennington." She was giggling when she hung up the phone, and it made him smile. He hoped that there would be other reasons to make her giggle. It sounded so good to him that he wanted to make her do it all the time.

Chapter 7

Knowing that there was a light at the end of the tunnel for her job, Rosie decided that working wasn't so bad. She didn't want to work, not at all right now, especially not as a cop, but she thought that she was handling things a lot better than before she gave her notice. The mayor was being extra nice to her, too, which she enjoyed. Being the chief and the mayor of such a small town, they'd butted heads quite often. Now it seemed like they were best of friends.

"I have two men on the way to be interviewed. One of them is coming out of retirement to take the job. He said that he could use the extra income and needed to get out of his house before his wife murdered him. I hope he was kidding." Rosie said she was sure that he had been. "The other interviewee is from Trinway. He's been out of the academy for a couple of years but works in Columbus as an officer. I don't know if he can take the small-town-ness of the area, so we'll have to keep an eye on him. It might be too boring for him to be around this small town. But if he grew up around here, maybe he'll be all right."

She'd been given files on both men and was

glad that he was going to be making her a part of the hiring process. She wasn't entirely sure she wanted to have much say, but she was glad for the input. Almost as soon as she opened the file on the younger man, she didn't think he'd be a good fit. Something about the way he looked in his picture turned her off from hiring him.

"Have you done background checks on them?" He told her that he thought that the academy had done that. "Both men haven't had a recent check. I'd do it just for peace of mind. You never know what's been going on in their lives since then."

"I never thought of that, and appreciate you pointing it out. I'll have them run tomorrow. Unless you can do it now." She said that she'd get right on it. "Good. Good. That'll save me some time in getting things set up for you. The town wants to interview them both, and I see no reason for that not to happen. We can have a town meeting and let them ask questions of the men that way. What do you think?"

"I think it could go either way. You might get someone like Mr. Henshaw there who will be asking them questions that have nothing to do with the jobs they're applying for. Or no one will show up." He said he was kind of hoping for the second of the two answers. "I would too. It could get out of hand quickly if there are so many people wanting answers. I'd play that by ear if I were you. As I said, it could go either way with them asking questions, so you never know what's going to be asked."

"I understand. And it's funny you should bring up old Howard. He is the one who wanted me to set up the meetings for them. I think he believes that he should have final say in who we hire simply because he's been around here the longest." She thought that was funny, but apparently it wasn't supposed to be. "I'll get back with you when the background checks come back. Just let me know."

She said that she would and called them in. Younger man McGee had to be called in twice, as they didn't have anyone by that name from the police academy. But she'd been spelling it wrong, so that had been the issue. By the time she was off the phone with the company that did them for the city, she was exhausted again. Happy for the reason, she took herself a little power nap and got on with her job.

Wylie came in to have lunch with her again. It was nice because he was getting her to eat instead of her eating through her time. Once she was finished with her burger and fries, she was tired again and thought that she could make it until the end of the day. Things were going well so far, and she was just happy to be able to be quitting sometime soon.

Getting a domestic call always scared her.

She knew that they were already volatile about the situation, and when the police showed up, things went twice as bad. Sending two of her men out on the call, she felt first guilty for sending them out, then relieved that she'd not have to be there if shots were fired. It went as easily as it usually did with this couple, and was happy that they were getting a divorce. They'd been at one another's throats since she started working for the town. And while it had been close before with them each having a gun, it made her nervous to go there since then.

By the time she was ready to go home, she'd filled out the required paperwork for her retirement. The HR department said that she could keep her insurance policy for personal life, and she decided that, since it was so little each month, she'd keep it. She didn't know what the future would hold, but knew that insurance was the way to go if you could get it. And she got to keep her group insurance for now, too.

Wylie had insurance through Meggie's work. She said that it started the day he'd been hired, and she was happy for that. The medical insurance from her job was good, but she was sure that Meggie's was better. She had a lot more people working for her, and the insurance would be cheaper. When the background checks came back, she called the mayor to tell him. He asked her straight up if McGee's had come back with anything negative on it.

"I've not read it over. I can if you want me to. I thought that the two of us were going over them together." He said he was on his way but wanted a heads-up. "If you're thinking that there is something wrong with him, then I'd not hire him. First impressions are what I always go by."

"There's a cockiness that he has that I don't care for. I also think, for some reason, he's going to want to change a lot of things. I don't think the people in this town are ready for someone to come in and change things around. Do you?" She said that they did have a lot of older people in their town who might be hurt by some changes. "You're very good at politics. You should run for my job when I'm up for reelection. Maybe not. I don't think I want to give up my job so quickly. I'm sort of established myself."

"I have no desire to have your job, sir. I'm leaving because I want to spend time with Wylie. We just bought a new home, and I'm excited to be able to make it a home. No, I have no desire to have your job. I think I'll have enough going on in my life to keep me busy." He asked about babies, and she was too startled to answer.

"They'll be coming along too someday, and you'll have your hands full with them. I love being a grandda, and I'm betting your parents will be thrilled with the prospect of bouncing them on their knees as well." She said that her mother was excited to have grandbabies. "Your daddy, too. He's a good man, and I'm sure that he's just busting at the seams until you tell him what you're having. Well, I'll be there soon. Look them over before I get there, and tell me something is wrong with McGee. I don't know why, but I just don't care for him."

She'd had the same feeling but didn't voice her concern with the mayor. It would matter to her being a citizen again in the town, and she didn't want to have to clash heads with someone after retiring. Rosie would if it came to that, but she didn't want to. It was hard enough leaving it to someone else. She didn't want to have to step in where she might not be wanted.

Both background checks came back good. She told the mayor as soon as he walked in, and she thought that he looked disappointed. She did point out that he was the one hiring him, and he had the final decision, but that didn't cheer him up much. Rosie was glad that she was going to be out of it sooner than she thought and didn't comment either way about the younger man.

After he left her, she put the checks into her file cabinet and locked the drawers. There really wasn't much in her office that she locked up, but she figured that she might as well put them away before it got around town about the two candidates for the job. She especially didn't want it to get around town who they were until it came time to interview them. The mayor had decided to have a question-and-answer session for the people of the town and let them be in on the get-go for hiring the new chief of police.

Taking a nap before Wylie got home, he still had to wake her up when he got there. She was all right with that. He woke her up in the most delicious way. Having dinner with him and the cook, she enjoyed her pasta and was glad that there was lots of sauce and bread to go with it. Her favorite thing to make while having spaghetti was garlic bread sandwiches. Stuffed by the time dinner was over, she decided to have dessert in the living room with Wylie. They'd been eating on a regular schedule now, and she was feeling better about it. All those nights when they ate at eleven or beyond had played havoc with her stomach.

They watched the news on their local channel, and she couldn't believe how much sports were on the station. She thought that it must be as boring a job as her own had been to be a news anchor locally. The sports guy was a little too much for her, and she muted the station so that she couldn't hear him. It was rude, she supposed, but she didn't care. It was her home, and she'd listen to what she wanted.

At ten, they were both in bed. They'd not made

love since she'd found out about the baby, and she wanted him. But as soon as she was in the bed, she was falling asleep. It didn't take much for her to want a nap before bedtime, and she didn't care what people thought. It was her body and her baby, and she'd do what was necessary to keep them both safe.

She'd noticed, too, that she seemed to be going to the bathroom a little more. Again, she wasn't worried about it as the doctor said her body was adjusting to all kinds of things and that would be one of them. He told her that she was going to be able to give birth easily because she was in such good shape. She didn't feel like she was until she woke from a nap, then she felt good. But this too would pass, she'd been told, and she was looking forward to having her energy back. She was tired of being exhausted all the time.

Getting up the second time, she was ready to face the day. But since it was only two in the morning, she thought that she might lie down for a while and rest. Going back to sleep wasn't a problem for her, and she was glad for that. In no time at all, she was sleeping again and didn't wake until her alarm went off at six-thirty.

It didn't take her long to get ready for work. She was having breakfast, another meal that she used to skip but was now having all the time. She was glad to see that Wylie was up and getting around by the time

she left. He was going to finish up his office in the Gold
building today, then he'd be able to start work when
she needed him. They were getting things squared
away, and she couldn't have been happier.

"I have to go into town tonight for a meeting
with the women's auxiliary club. I'm not sure what it's
about, but they requested that Kinsey and I attend. It's
not a meal, but those little plates stuff so I won't be
home in time for dinner. Make sure you eat." She told
him that she would; she liked being able to have things
just so. "Good. You don't seem to be sleeping as much,
and I'm glad. I miss you when you nap, but I do love
watching you sleep. You're beautiful."

"Thank you. I needed to hear that about now."
As they finished up their meal, she didn't feel as
exhausted as she'd been lately. She hoped that it was
passing, this need to sleep all the time, but time would
tell. She was just glad to be able to spend more time with
Wylie that didn't have her sleeping on his shoulder.
Not that he ever complained, but she was glad that he
was there for her. She loved him very much.

At ten, they were headed to bed. She'd not
been asleep all evening and thought that was a great
accomplishment. Not that she wasn't tired, but she
was staying awake so that she could go to bed with
Wylie. She knew that he was getting up after she
went to sleep and was all right with that. He wasn't

as exhausted as she was, and she loved him for taking that into consideration when he got up. She really did love that man so much.

~*~

Ara had been observing his brothers for the past month. They were all doing the same thing and spending money like they still didn't have any. The only one that wasn't as bad was Wylie, but he would spend money on discount stores or clearance items instead of buying what he could afford. And they all could afford a great deal more than they were spending.

He noticed that David would carry around hundreds of dollars with him at all times. So he thought that he'd try it. It didn't work out well for him or anyone around him. Ara had made a fool of himself trying to be the rich man, and he thought perhaps he'd never tell anyone what had happened.

Putting two hundred dollars in his wallet, he felt good. While he was home. But as soon as he got out in public, he would check his wallet several times a minute to make sure that he hadn't lost it. Or someone hadn't taken it. As the day wore on, he was fearful of bumping into people for fear of them being the best pickpockets around. He made himself sick with worrying about the money he had on him, and it got to the point where he'd not even take out his change to pay for a soda for fear of someone robbing him. People stared at him, too. He was sure that it was all his fault because he'd been acting like a lunatic. He even found himself eyeing people hard who would bump into him, then checking for his wallet. By the time he got himself home with his money, he had to dry heave several times because he'd made himself that worried over the money. It was only two hundred dollars, too. He wondered what would happen to him if he'd had more on him. He didn't even want to think about that.

Understanding didn't make it any better. They'd been without money for most of their lives, well into their adulthood. And not that they didn't have money for fries when they had a hamburger, they didn't have the money to drive to the place to get either one. They were on the road to disaster every day, and he wondered why he couldn't carry around some money. It's small wonder that any of them could even find themselves a house with as much money as it took to buy one. But then that wasn't on them; perhaps that was it.

Ara still worked for the newspaper in town. There wasn't much ever going on with it, so he had time to speculate on things like money and people. He knew that people did treat them differently since they'd sold the farm. It was like they expected them to go around paying for everything that needed to be done, like the new school.

There had been enough money for the new school to be built. Plenty enough is what he'd heard, but they wanted more donations so that they could have some of the state-of-the-art teaching tools that would make them get better students from around the state.

When they'd help out a family, it wasn't for the money that they could give them. Many of them didn't have anymore than they did. But now, when they wanted someone to help them, they'd talk about being paid. Like if I have you work for me, I'm going to expect you to pay me too. So far, he'd been told that several times.

Like he'd been out writing a story on one of the families that had hit on harder times. While he was interviewing them, the man had asked for a hundred bucks to get the real story. He didn't think it was right to pay for a story and turned him down. The man tossed him out of the house then and said he wasn't going to give him anything that he'd profit from. Like working for a job was profit.

He supposed it was for him. Ara liked working, and it gave him some pocket money. It wasn't a great deal, just enough to take himself out to dinner one night or to buy him a book that he'd been wanting to read. He didn't waste it on things like games of chance or things like that. He just spent it to make himself feel better. And working did that for him, too.

Being idle had never been something that he enjoyed. Even when there was no story coming into work, he would find things to do around the building. It was why the entire backlog of papers had been cleaned top to bottom. He couldn't stand to be sitting around waiting for the next big story to come through. He supposed that's why he was able to stay on when others would be fired. He kept himself useful.

"Hello, Ara. How's it going?" He smiled at Mr. Howard, the banker, and told him he was doing just fine. "You looking for a house too? I'm to understand that your other brothers are going to find them something sooner rather than later. That makes for a nice income for the city when there are a number of houses going to be sold. Helps with the schools, too, I'm to understand."

"I've not decided what I'm going to do yet. I did rent a condo with the others. With Meggie having a baby, we didn't want to intrude on their time as a couple." He told him that it was jolly good. The man was nice but an oddball of sorts. "I'm thinking I'm going to wait until the new year to decide what I'm going to be doing when it comes to getting a house."

"There are two that just came to the bank." He didn't know what that meant, so he waited for him to tell him. "Foreclosure is a terrible thing, but we have to do it in order to make money for ourselves. The bank can't make it on promises and bounced check fees. No sir. We have to have income coming in, too."

"I understand. He really didn't, but thought that if he were to talk to the man much longer, he'd understand. He seemed to be in a talkative mood today. "Who have you foreclosed on? Someone from around town?"

Foreclosure. That word he knew. They'd been terrified of it happening to them the entire time he'd been living on the farm. The bank could and would come in and take it all away from you. Your house, land, clothing, and anything that might have been left behind. They didn't care what it meant to you; if they could get a dollar for it, it was going to be put up for sale so that they could get their money back from you forfeiting in a deal you had with the bank.

He realized that he'd missed something when Howard had been talking. Asking him to repeat himself seemed rude since he'd asked the question, he only nodded his head and told him that it was a shame. Smiling, Howard told him that one man's problems could be a gain for him. He didn't know if he could buy a house that had been foreclosed on. The people might still be around town, and that he'd never be able to live down. Buying a property that had had a family in it that he knew. That was why he was so keen on building a home. No one had lived it in before him, and he knew that it wasn't going to be someone's livelihood that he was profiting on. He thought that he needed to get his head together before he started giving all his money away so that he'd feel better.

He decided to go and see David. He'd give him advice on how to combat these feelings of being too rich. Making his way to his car, he even thought about how none of his brothers had brought a new car when they had the money to do so. Not even himself. Shaking his head, he made his way to the farm to see how the best man he knew was dealing with being a billionaire.

David wasn't home, but Alice was, and she fixed him a cup of tea to go with the cookies that she'd just baked while he poured out his story. He had skipped around a couple of times, but she said that she understood what he was saying. When she finally sat down, he waited for her to tell him he was being foolish.

"The house that we gave your brother was foreclosed on. Someone who had been friends with us, as a matter of fact. We tried to help them, but they wouldn't have it. Their pride got them into trouble, and it was keeping them from getting the help that they needed to save their home. I'm sure that the bank tried to work with them, too, as they don't want to foreclose on anyone. There's not just a lot of paperwork to be filled out, but they might not get what they want from the house in the end." He said that he'd not thought about that. "I'm sure if you were to ask Mr. Howard about it, he'd tell you the same thing. That the people just wouldn't play ball with them, and that's what made them lose their homes."

He told her about how he'd been trying to spend money and hadn't gotten the hang of it yet. She told him that it was a good thing. That they'd have money well beyond their lives, and that would be a good nest egg for their children.

"I'm not sure that I want to have a family. I don't know why, but I think there are enough people in the world who have children they can't afford." She said she wished they'd had children. "I'm sorry. I had forgotten about that. I didn't mean to make you feel bad."

"I'm all right. Today. Some days are worse than others. But I have to tell you that having you six around, coming to us for advice, has been the best thing that has happened to us. We just love you all like you're our own children." She laughed. "We've even thought about adopting the six of you, but you're a might old to be calling us mom and dad at this late in the game."

"I was just a kid when my mom was killed by our father. Did someone tell you that he died in prison?"

She said that she'd heard about it from Kinsey. "He goes to you for advice all the time he told me. I love having you guys around to help us. What I was getting at, I'd love to call you mom. You're the best thing that has happened to us since I was a child. And I couldn't ask for a better role model."

She got up and turned her back to him. He could tell that she was crying, and it hurt him in his heart that he'd caused her to do that. Getting up, he pulled her into his arms and held her while she sobbed. His own eyes filled with tears as he held her in his arms while she cried. He wondered what he'd do if she were to tell one of his brothers that he'd made her cry. They'd more than likely kill him.

After a bit, she stopped crying, but he continued to hold her. She laid her head on his shoulder and told him he was a good man. He thought that she couldn't have given him a better compliment than that, and he was proud to have her say that to him.

Sitting down when she said she was all right, he enjoyed another cookie. He didn't much care for the tea, preferring a nice glass of milk instead. He drank it with the cookies and didn't say anything. She'd been kind to him, and he hoped someday that he'd be able to repay her for her kindness. The Winchesters really were the best part of selling the farm to them. They'd become close friends, and it felt good to have someone in his corner all the time.

Being invited to stay for dinner, he couldn't find it in him to turn her down. They were having steaks on the grill, and it was his favorite meal. David arrived home around four, and they sat in the living room of their new home and talked about what he'd talked to Alice about earlier. He got a kick out of the story about having money on him and how it had made him sick. He related his own story about money, too, that had him laughing hard.

"I'd been about seventeen and wanted to show up that I had some money. I didn't. I was just beginning to show my worth to my father when I wanted to be a big man. So I went to the bank and got myself two stacks of ones. They made my wallet look fatter, you see. When I pulled out one of the tens I had too, I made sure that they could all see that I had a wad of cash. Little did I know I was showing them that I had all ones while I was at it. It took me making my first million before I got over that. Today, I carry around money so that I know that I can spread it around. What I love doing now that I'm making my own way in the world." Ara said he'd have to do that, so he'd feel better if he were to lose his wallet. "No, don't do that. You be who you are, young man, and you'll be just fine. If you can't spend your money on things that you want, you're going to regret it. Find a passion and fill your home with it. Even if it's making puzzles. You do what makes you feel good."

He was going to do just that. As soon as he figured out what made him happy. Right now, he was able to afford the things that he needed when he needed them. He knew that before long, he'd find what made him happy. The first thing that popped into his head was traveling. He wanted to see the world, but he'd start with the country that he was in. He'd not seen much of it since he'd been a kid and wanted that more than anything. As soon as he found himself a house, he was going to travel around, finding new adventures to tell his family about someday. Yes, he thought, that's just what he was going to do.

He'd figure out a plan and go for it. It would be an eye-opener because he'd only been in Ohio all his life and wanted to try different foods. See different things while he was out and have some fun, and spend a little bit of his money. He might even get himself a truck and a tent to go on his camping trips and do that. He was excited about going around to the different states and was going to start on his planning as soon as he got home.

Chapter 8

Wylie felt like a man on top of the world today. He'd made love to Rosie for the first time since finding out about the baby, and it had been epic. The way that the two of them came together was something that he'd love her for the rest of their life. It was gentle in a consuming sort of way, and he wanted that sort of passion all the time.

He'd been woken up by coming down her throat. She'd been having her way with him for some time if his cock being painfully hard had any indication. When he begged her to let him fuck her, she said that she was having too much fun and that he should go back to sleep. Like that was ever going to happen. As fucked her mouth, he guided her with his hand to where it felt the best. She was doing such a wonderful job that he held off coming until he couldn't stand it anymore while she sucked him.

When she cupped his balls gently in her hands, he nearly came up off the bed. It wasn't painful, not at all; it was the pleasure that was painful to his cock. Coming again, crying out with it, he knew that if he didn't have her soon, he was going to die from it.

Pulling her up his body, he'd made sure that she knew that he needed her by kissing her savagely. Then, as he was going to take her, a gentleness settled over him, and he made love to her slowly. She seemed to have needed it as well because she didn't complain about how he'd changed up his making love to her.

Touching her where he could, he kissed her softly. As she moaned at times, he felt his cock harden even more, but did not need to take control. He slid into her then fucked her just as slowly. When she came several times, one right after the other, he made sure that she enjoyed it as much as he did, making love to her. Taking her hands to the top of the bed, he held them there as he kissed her again. Touching her breast, he was amazed at how it filled his hand, and her nipple became so hard. When he finally came with her, she cried out, digging her nails into his back, holding onto him. As he emptied into her for the final time, he dropped atop of her and laid there. He was spent and couldn't move. It wasn't until she started to wiggle out from under him that he was able to move off her and to the side of the bed. It was nice having a bed big enough for this kind of lovemaking. He'd pay twice what he'd paid for it just to be able to lay on his side and touch Rosie in the aftermath of their loving.

"I have to get up." He asked her why, it was Saturday. "I have that meeting with the townspeople today about my replacement. I have a feeling that they're going to go with McGee, as he is the most charismatic person I've met. If I didn't know it was all for show, I'd believe the shit that he's telling."

"What kind of stuff is he peddling? I'm sure that some people will be able to see right through him." She said that people wanted new and younger. "You're younger. Why on earth would you say that about yourself?"

"I mean over Peterson. He's been retired longer than I've been working as a cop, and I don't see him being up to date on things that would be important to the town." She got up and stood at the side of the bed. "I'm not sure I'd go with Peterson either, but of the two of them, McGee scares me a bit. I have a feeling that he's going to be one of those cops who follow every rule to the letter and not let anyone slide like I did. It's going to be tough for everyone in town."

"Do you know this about him, or are you just guessing? I'm not sure about the man other than what you've told me. I think I'd be scared of him as well." He got up himself and went to turn on the shower for her. "People don't like change, and if he does too much of it right off the bat, he's going to be out of a job before he even gets to decorate his office to his liking."

Rosie laughed and said that he'd come in on Thursday and was measuring her office. He thought that was a little cheeky and told her so. She told him that he was also filling out a list of things that he wanted to do on his first day in office.

"I'm sure that it's not going to go over well for either one of them. I guess we'll have to be watching ourselves from now on. Not that I remember doing all that much wrong in the first place, but I don't want to spend any time in jail. Not when I just got my life together. I love sleeping with you in our big bed. I don't think I'd do well with a little cot and you not around." He pouted for her, making her laugh. "That's just what I wanted. You to laugh for me. It might not be as bad as you think. Hopefully not anyway. I guess we'll have to just wait and see what he does."

"I don't like it. Nor him. There is something else about him that I don't care for, and I can't put my finger on it right now. It's like he's testing me sometimes when he's in the office. I don't know. Perhaps he'll be just fine, and it's my hormones that are making me see something that's not there." Wylie trusted her opinion over anything else. If she didn't like the guy, then there was a reason for it. She'd never said that to him in all the time they'd been together. "I'm going to take a shower, and then I'm going to the school. I did tell you that's where they're having the meet and greet, right? It was the biggest place we could get into. I have a feeling that most of the town will show up for this thing even if they don't have anything to say."

After she got into the shower, he made the bed. It was something that he was in the habit of doing and hadn't gotten out of it yet. He didn't know if he wanted to. It felt good to have his bed made when he went to breakfast. He also picked up the laundry around the room and put it in the basket as well. He was getting good, he thought at being a domestic worker at home.

When he got out of his shower and dressed, he headed down to the kitchen. Rosie was just finishing up hers when a plate of food was set in front of him. He ate while talking to both Rosie and their cook about dinner tonight. He wanted pork chops, and that sounded all right with Rosie. The cook, her name was Linda, said she'd have them ready at six and would have bread to do with it. He was happy for the bread. He loved her warm bread with butter all over it.

Today, he was meeting his brothers for lunch. They were getting together once a week and on Saturday afternoon so that they could have the rest of the day to hang out. This was their second lunch meeting, and so far, he was having a good time. He saw most of them every day and caught up with them. But having a time when they could get together was fantastic because there just didn't seem to be enough time to talk about their lives when they were running around working. He thought that they all had a job, including Kinsey now, and they seemed to be happier for it.

"I've been looking at the stocks that we have with David. Did you know that he's hired extra people so that they can work with us? I thought that was wonderful of him to do that. I know that I trust his word over anyone else's when it comes to trading and buying." He told Raphael that he'd not known that, but felt bad that he was footing the bill. "Yeah, I thought of that too, but I figured that if he didn't want to do it, he'd say so. One thing that I've learned from David is that when he doesn't want to do something, he has no trouble telling you no. He's not done it to me, but I've heard him tell others no. He does it in a way that there are no feelings hurt either."

"Alice is the same way. She's much nicer at it than David is. While still getting her point across, she almost makes you think you're the one who decided not to do it instead of her telling you that she didn't want to. Understand?" He laughed and said that he did. "Good. I love her. I've started calling her mom lately. She loves it, and I feel good about it too."

"I've slipped up and called them both mom or dad once or twice. They've been better parents than our own had been. And even though dad never hit us, he made sure we understood that he could if he wanted to. Did you ever hear anything more from the prison?"

He said that he'd not and figured that whatever he had with him when he died went with him in the grave. "That's what I thought too. He was never one to hoard things anyway. I do remember that about him. If it didn't mean anything to him, he'd toss it out."

"Yeah, I got that too." They talked around the table about what was going on in their lives and found out that his brothers were going to be buying a home soon. "The bank told you about two houses that are coming on the market? Well, that's great. I didn't know that the bank could do that."

"They own the houses after foreclosure and can do with them what they want if they want to." Wylie didn't know that, but Ara seemed to know a great deal about them. He'd been the one who had told him that he'd been calling Alice mom. So he'd done it a couple of times just to test the waters. He didn't have a problem with it, and neither did she. "I thought about buying one of them, but decided that I'm going to build. I've thought about it, and I want to have my own things in my first house. I think I'd enjoy picking out the cabinets too."

School had started a couple of days ago, and the kids were off the streets now. He'd been seeing less and less of them over the past week. Getting ready, he supposed. But Kinsey had told him that football was starting and that the kids were practicing. He loved that time of year when he'd been a kid. He'd work out a little each day so that he could be in better shape before they started. But he was still huffing and puffing by the time the first time rolled around. That was one of his fondest memories of being a kid was the practice after school.

He had other memories of high school that were fond to him. His grandda and grannie going to every game they played in too. Wylie had been the only one who had been the quarterback because he'd been so tall. The others had played linebacker, and he loved that they were there for him every time he made a play. The Pennington boys had made their mark on the field and off it when they'd been playing. Grannie had made sure that they had plenty to eat, too, so that they'd not fall ill with all the workouts.

They talked about what they were going to be doing in the winter months. That used to be the time when they'd make sure that their equipment lasted for another spring to fall. Also, it would be the time that they'd harvest their garden. For the six of them, it was nice having a garden that they could use to supplement their food bills.

The six of them had joined up when they got out of high school. Kinsey, of course, had been first, and when he got out, he was right behind him in getting out, too. They'd each gotten an education by being in the service, and he knew that it helped their grannie when they'd send her their paycheck when they got it. They all had done something with their education, too. He and Kinsey had both made sure they knew how to take on tasks with the farm, and the others had done the same. Ara had gotten himself a journalist education, and he'd been able to help the farm by working for the local newspaper. He wished his grannie were alive to see how much things had come to fruition for them all.

They talked about her now and again. She was the biggest part of their lives after their mother had been killed. She never said a word about not being able to raise them, being as old as she and grandda had been, but gathered them up after the funeral and welcomed them to the farm. They would work hard for their daily bread, and Grannie always made sure that they had plenty to eat and wear when the time came for them to work the farm for her. Then grandda had died. He'd gotten a cold one fall day and had died the following winter. He'd been sorely missed since then, and he was glad that they'd had them both when they did.

During lunch, Kinsey passed around the seed catalog that he'd gotten in the mail. It was funny to them all to go over it the way that they did when they were struggling. Kinsey would do the final order, but he always asked for their input. It was the way he loved beets as much as he did because one year Kinsey had asked if they wanted anything different, and he'd suggested beets. Every year since then, it had been added to the garden just for him, as the others didn't care for them. It was memories like that one that made him love his brothers so much. They'd really been together on things that had affected them, and he couldn't have been happier with them.

After lunch, they decided to go to the meeting. It had started at one, and they were about twenty minutes late. He'd not told them about McGee and Rosie not liking him. He figured that he'd let them decide for themselves. It was unanimous by the time the meeting was over that, first of all, he was going to be the new chief of police, and that no one in his family liked him.

~*~

Rosie didn't have to stay on and train the new man who was taking her place. She said she'd do it until he decided that he knew all there was to know. He had brought in new men to work for the department, which didn't surprise her. But it was the way that he talked about layoffs that bothered her. After the second day of not doing anything, she decided that she'd had enough and told him to call her if he had any questions. He told her that he had it all, and that was fine with her. She was going to go home, put her feet up, and not worry about the department anymore. They'd made their choice, and now they were going to have to live with it.

As she was making her way home with her box of things from her desk, she passed by a couple that she'd not met before. They said they were visiting their town and were into the baskets. She knew that they were famous for being the basket capital of the world, or so she'd been told, but she didn't know how much of that was going on anymore. There were still shops, but not nearly as many as there used to be when the company was doing well. Wishing them luck, she was putting her things in her car when the man came back to her.

"I've heard that there are other baskets being made in town. Do you know anything about them?" She told him how to get to the new basket shop and thought that would be the end of it. "Can't you just take us there? We've been walking all day, and our feet are killing us."

"I'm sorry, but I can't do that. I have to get home. It's just down the block." He seemed pissed off at her and told her that it would be the friendly thing to do. "I'm sorry, but no. I've got to get home."

The slap to her face startled her, and she knew that he'd drawn blood. While she was trying to get her bearings, he opened her car door, putting her box on the ground, and shut the door. Like she was going to take him anywhere after that. Picking up her box of things, she put them in the trunk and made her way into the office again. She was just telling one of the officers what had happened when McGee showed up.

"They hit you? For no reason?" She had to explain how she'd told them that she wasn't going to take them to the basket shop, and he seemed confused. "It's not like you have a job or anything. Why didn't you just take them?"

"Because I've got to get home." He actually rolled his eyes at her, and she pulled out her cell phone. Calling Wylie, she told him what was going on. "So if you could come and get me and take me to the clinic or hospital, I'd like a record of the man hitting me."

"I'll be right there. Don't kill anyone." She thought that was sound advice if she still had her gun, but it was in her box of things to take home. "I love you, babe."

Finally convincing the police that she was serious about pressing charges against the man, she was happy when someone went out and got them out of her car. They were bitching and cursing when they'd been brought in, and she couldn't believe that they were blaming her for not taking them when she had a car right there to do so. People weren't nice when they were in a touristy town, and she should have remembered that.

She not only pressed charges against the man, Mr. Manner of all things, but she'd also told them that since they'd hit her and taken her car, she wanted to press charges for that as well. McGee went to his office like he didn't want to be associated with the deed, and she filled out the paperwork herself. The little shit was going to have to learn the laws if he was going to be able to take on this town.

Both of them were arrested, and that didn't go over well with McGee. He wanted to have a nice, calm town and wasn't sure why she was upsetting the apple cart so soon after he'd taken over her job. She'd been assaulted, and her car had been confiscated, and she wanted justice. Wylie showed up just as she was being looked at by the medic in town. She was going to the hospital so that there would be a record of what had happened in the event that it went to court.

"I'm going to have to kill that man, you know that, don't you?" She asked him if he was kidding, and he didn't even blink at her. "He hit you for no other reason than you told him no. I can't believe that there are still people like that in the world. He should have been slapped around as well. And then there is McGee. The little shit is on my list now, and I have the power to get him into trouble. You're well-liked in this town, and people are going to be up in arms about how you were treated. Not just by the Manners but also the chief."

She had to get three stitches in her cheek and was surprised that they didn't just tape it together. But they said that it would leave a nasty scar, and she didn't need that. As soon as she was released, they got them some dinner as it was getting late. She wanted a burger and fries, and he wanted a milkshake. They were at the best little burger place in town when she heard from David.

"I heard that you'd been hurt. I wish you would have called me." She told him that there hadn't been any time, as she had been hurt and went to the hospital within an hour. "I still would have liked to have known. Next time, have Wylie call me first thing. I love you like a daughter, and I hate that I couldn't be there for you when you might have needed me."

"I'm going home soon. We decided to have some dinner out, and then I'm going home to be pampered." He said that she deserved it more than most. "Thank you for that. I'm sure that Wylie will give me his best while I'm at home. I'm finished working for the department now, and I couldn't be happier."

"I don't care for the little pisser. He was rude to me when I asked about what had happened to you. He told me that you were making it out to be something more than it was and that he was upset with you. He's not the one who had to have stitches, so I will take care of him soon enough." She asked him what he meant, hoping that he wasn't going to confess to killing him, too. "I have the backing of a great deal of money. When I want something, I get it. And I want this little pisser out of office as of right now."

"Just don't do anything that will get you into trouble. You mean a great deal to me, and I'd hate to visit you in prison for something so trivial as me getting a few stitches." She wondered how he'd found out and decided that she didn't want to know. With money came power, and David seemed to have a great deal of both. "I'm not going to tell you not to worry because I can tell that you already are, but I'm fine. As soon as I get home, I'm going to really put my feet up and take a nap. I deserve it, I believe."

"Yes, you do, honey. And if Wylie doesn't pamper you enough, you know to call me. I'll be there with a masseuse to do the job." They both laughed, but she did wonder if he was serious. The man rarely joked about things, and she thought that he wasn't kidding now. "All right, I'm going to let you go. The next time you want to take on a visitor to our town, give me a call. I'll make sure he knows that you're not to be messed with."

"I will, I promise." After putting her phone back in her pocket, she enjoyed the rest of her meal.

The burger was perfect, and she loved the shoestring fries that she'd gotten to go with it. After taking a few sips of Wylie's malt, she decided that she couldn't eat another bite and pushed her plate away. She knew that she'd have to wait until she got home to nap, but she could curl up in the booth they were in and sleep for a month. The stress of the day made her exhausted again. "I've been doing so well at not sleeping as much, but today wore me out. First, dealing with the little pisser, and secondly, the Manners. Do you suppose they figured that their name gave them special privileges or something? I wouldn't put it past them. I bet they're just loved to pieces in their own town. To imagine that they'd think that was all right with a person to be slapped like they were nothing."

"Like you said, I'm betting that they're used to getting their way, and when you told them no, they resorted to violence." He kissed the area close to her stitches and told her that he loved her. "I'm going to take you home, and you're going to nap on the couch until it's bedtime. Tomorrow you're off, and while I'm gone, I want you to make sure you rest as much as you can so that you're well rested when I get home. I might want to make love to you again."

"You always want to make love. I wonder how I keep up." They both laughed, and she decided that she'd had enough being pissed off at McGee. He wasn't her problem anymore, and she didn't want to have to deal with him anymore. If he needed help from her, which she didn't see him asking for, she was going to tell him to fuck off. It was the least she could do to him after the way that he treated her today. The little pisser.

True to his word, Wylie pampered her every bit as much as she needed. He not only massaged her feet for her, but he also made sure she had a cup of hot cocoa so that she could enjoy her nap. Cocoa always put her to sleep, and now was no different. As soon as she closed her eyes, she was out.

Waking up at ten, she wondered how she was ever going to get to sleep tonight. But as usual, she was fighting sleep even as she laid in bed waiting for Wylie to join her. As soon as he wrapped her up in his arms, she decided that there wasn't a better place to be than where she was right now. But when she saw the lights go out, she thought of the man who had hit her.

"He really didn't care that I was a woman getting off work." Wylie told her that his type of people rarely cared about anything but their own wants and needs. "I get that, but he actually hit me like I was his child or something. I wonder if they have any kids? I'm betting that they have very little to do with them. I'd certainly not."

"You never know. It could have been a one-time

thing with him being cranky about his poor feet. I'm not taking his side in this, but he might have figured that he was in a tourist town and that rules didn't apply to him. I've seen that happen before." She looked at him in the dark room. She asked him when. "Once when I was in town with Kinsey, we were loading up some feed for the chickens when this man came up to us and asked us about what sort of farm animals we had on our farm. Being nice, we told him, but didn't stop what we were doing. The man said, not asked, but told us that we were to allow his kids to come out to the farm and pet our animals. Like that would be something that we'd do."

"What happened? You didn't take him up on his so generous offer, did you?" He laughed and told her no, that they'd not. Then he told her what had happened. "They called the police on you? What a shitty thing to do. I'm hoping that whoever was in charge told them no as well."

"He couldn't believe that they thought that was something we should have been arrested for. I think it was the guy before you, old man Hamilton. He just stared at them for so long that I was sure that he was having a stroke or something. Anyway, he just walked away without even bothering to talk to the man. To this day, I think about that and wonder what would have happened if someone else had been in charge. We never took them out to the farm, nor did his kids get to pet any animals either. I can't believe that they thought it would be all right with us that they petted the cows. Damn it, but people are strange."

She snuggled down under the covers with Wylie and closed her eyes. She was really tired even though she'd had a nice nap. Tomorrow was going to be the first day of the rest of her life without working as a chief, and she was looking forward to it more than she might have thought about this morning. Wylie was right; people were strange.

Chapter 9

"Were you a part of this?" Hailey shook her head no, but didn't put her hands down. She liked every part of her body without holes in it. And the police were just itching to plug a few holes into someone. "Well, someone was in on it, and I want answers. Who started this and why?"

"I came into this just about the time you did, sir." He snorted at her, an honest-to-goodness snort, and moved away. She'd not been kidding. She was coming into the building when about fifty police officers came into the room right behind her, shoving her ahead all the way. If there had been anyone shooting at them, she would have been first in line to have a bullet in her head.

They were all dressed in dark uniforms with helmets on, as well as gloves. She wondered briefly if the gloves were bulletproof, but didn't want to seem like she was too interested in their clothing, for she might end up dead like the man lying beside her. The police hadn't shot him, but he was dead for sure.

There was a woman across from her who was winking and tilting her head like she knew something.

Ignoring her as best she could, Hailey looked around the room that once held a nice kitchen. She didn't know what had gone on before she'd gotten here, but something big had gone down, and she was in the dark as to what. She had a feeling that winker knew, but she wasn't going to ask her. She just needed to get out of here before anything else happened.

The officer who had told her to kneel down and shut up stood in front of her. His gun was laying across his chest, and he was holding it like he was ready to use it. He asked her name. Clearing her throat twice, she was finally able to squeak it out.

"Hailey Sheppard. I work here." He nodded once and moved on. Kicking the dead man, she wondered if he was trying to get his name, too. "That's Jamie Sheppard. No relation. He works...worked here too. We did the dishes together."

"Why's he dead?" She thought he was asking her for the cause of death, and she told him someone had shot him in the head. "I know that, dumbass. I was wondering why someone killed the dishwasher. And how did you make it out if he was bent on killing everyone in the place."

"I just got here. Just as you people were coming in, you shoved me on down the hall and past the time clock so that I couldn't clock in." She looked up at the man. "I don't have a clue what's going on right now other than the place I work looks like a bloodbath."

"You just keep your mouth shut, and you might make it to the time clock. Though I doubt anyone will care that you've been late today." She could see that. Her boss was sitting in his office chair with his head blown off. The only reason she knew it was him was because he always wore a lot of gold chains, and the headless man had several on that looked like something he wore. It was making her sort of sick to see all this blood, but she was going to hang on to her breakfast if it was the last thing she did today. "When they ask for information, you tell them to come and look for Chief of Police McGee."

"And who would that be?" He pointed to himself, and she could see that he was pissed off that she hadn't known who he was. "I'll tell them. Do you suppose they'll care?"

"They'd better." She'd make sure they knew who to look for when they started asking her questions, but she didn't know what good it would do. She didn't much care for the Chief, but she'd do as she was told. When he moved on, she finally sat down on her feet. Sitting up the way that she'd been was hurting her toes and knees. And with her hands up and over her head like they were, she was beginning to cramp up in the worst sort of ways.

She sat there stretching as best she could without

causing anyone to look in her direction. Winker was still at it, and she finally turned around to see if there was someone behind her that she was trying to get the attention of. Nope. Just her. Or Jamie. But he wasn't getting it either.

Hailey thought about what Jamie had told her a few months ago. About the restaurant that they both were working for. He'd been here for about five years, and she'd been here for about three. It was coming up on her anniversary in a few weeks. He said that he thought the place was going to go up in a blaze of glory soon. She didn't know what that meant, nor did she care, but it looked to her like someone had tried to do what he'd predicted.

There were two more bodies that she could see. One was the hostess, and the other had been Mary Sue, one of the waitresses. She couldn't see what had killed them, but they were dead as Jamie because she'd seen all the blood.

Then there was Winker. She didn't know where she worked, but she did have on one of the uniforms of the people who worked in the kitchen. Her hair was stringy, and her face looked like she'd taken some kind of scrub brush to it, but other than that, she looked all right. She looked like she'd not had a proper bath in about a year. Plus, she was super skinny, like food was way down on her list of things to partake in. The man

McGee came back.

"You can let her go." He pointed his gun at her, and she looked at the man with him. "She doesn't know anything, and I don't like the way she keeps looking around. Take her up front and get her particulars so we can contact her when we need something."

She assumed that her particulars were her home address and phone number. She'd give that to him, but she wasn't going to be staying here for long. Jamie had told her that when the place went up, to find a place to hide until it was over. While she didn't have a clue what he'd been talking about, she was going to run for cover as soon as she was out of here. Things that he'd told her were coming out, and she wanted nothing to do with the place.

When she was allowed to stand, she had to hold onto the table behind her for several minutes. She'd been sitting in that position for about twenty or so minutes, and she hurt from it. Hailey was used to being on her feet all day, but this had been something different.

Hailey was also used to disappearing. When she was a child, it was what she did the best when there was trouble in the house. Not only could she disappear in the house, but she could not see her parents for weeks before she let them see her. They didn't seem to mind, however, and she was fine with that too. Then, as she got older, she was even better at getting lost, so that when people came around to her family home, they would sometimes be surprised that they even had a child. Hailey liked that most of all.

After giving them her address and phone number, she was allowed to leave. Going out of the big building, she took out her cell phone, took out the SIM card, and busted the phone. As she walked past her car, she got two bags out of her trunk and kept walking toward the line of trees that was behind the restaurant. If anyone had been watching, they'd think she'd been swallowed up by the trees.

Getting about five miles from the restaurant, she stopped long enough to see what she had in her backpack. There was money in one of them, her checks from the last few months cashed and lying in neat stacks. She had food enough to get her by this evening, but she'd have to find something that would tide her over until tomorrow night. Plus, she had several changes of clothing that would do her for a while and a wig. It had seen better days, but she was going to use it only if necessary. And today it felt like it might be more necessary than ever before.

She'd been prepared for this for the last six months. Jamie told her to be ready to go. That as soon as the place was gone—he'd never said how it would be gone, but he did tell her there would be fire—she was to light out like the police were after her and she'd stolen the biggest gem on this side of the United States. She took him at his word.

Now she was on the run and without much in the way of information. She had an idea what had gone on at the restaurant, but not knowing if she was right or not, she kept her mouth shut. She'd thought that the restaurant was doing too well to be out in the middle of nowhere and without the customers that seemed to be avoiding the place. She did the dishes; she knew how many people were eating at the place nightly.

"Fentanyl." She had figured that was what Jamie was trying his best not to tell her about it. The entire ground floor of the place had been closed for years. She figured that there must have been about thirty workers down there, from the cars that were always in the lot, and that they were making and selling the fentanyl right out the front door.

Her boss, Mr. Shadows, certainly not his real last name, seemed to have wads of cash on him all the time. When the restaurant ran out of something, he'd peel a few hundred off of his pocket and tell Jamie to take the company van and run to the store and get it. It didn't matter what it was, either, from steaks to lettuce. He'd come back with the van loaded up, and she'd have to help him unload it all.

She never seen enough people in the place to

justify that amount of food coming in, but she kept her mouth shut. Jamie would talk to her on breaks. And his stories would terrify her to no end about what was going to happen to the place should the police or someone who had more firepower come along and decide that they'd had enough. Enough what, she would never know unless it was in the paper, but she was glad to have been able to get away from the place before anyone wanted answers from her. She didn't have any.

The little town where she lived was perfect for where she wanted to go. They'd notice a stranger in town, which was why, for the past six months, she'd made sure that she'd been seen by just about everyone around. She'd even taken jobs that were there just so she'd have a presence in town. Not knowing what was going on, she made sure that she'd be able to hide in plain sight when the time came to disappear.

She'd even known that McGee was the new chief of police in town, and he didn't even realize that she'd babysat his kids one night recently. She was good at making herself hide out and had done it for so long that she was sure that she could do it for the rest of her life and not be caught.

Hailey decided that she could go into the greenhouse to spend a couple of days. There had been work started on it earlier in the year, but it had stopped. There was heat in the place now, for which she was grateful, and figured that she could stay in it for the rest of the fall and into winter. She'd already gotten herself a post office box with her name on it. All she had to do was collect it once a week, and that would be another place that people would see her at.

Situating herself in the greenhouse office, she was able to use the big bags of soil for a bed. They weren't as soft as a bed, but they were warm with the heat of the office that she'd carried them into. In addition to a bed, she also had herself a table with the desk and a little heater that someone had left behind. There was even a hot plate that she could use, but she was slightly afraid of it. The plug was frayed, and she didn't trust the wiring around it. She would only use it if she were there all the time. She didn't want to burn down the place just because she wanted her soup hot.

Fixing herself some ramen noodles for dinner, she was set up about as well as she could be and still have food and water. After taking an inventory of the place and then figuring out different ways to get in and out, she felt that she was safe here until spring. She didn't know if they were going to start the greenhouse up again or if they'd abandon it, as it looked to her like they had.

The next morning, she didn't even bother trying to look for a newspaper. It only came out once a week, and she'd be lucky if the news in it wasn't about a month old. Mostly, it kept up with the local sports teams and what they were doing, but it rarely, if ever, had a front page that would tell you something that you'd need to know, like a restaurant that had been shot up and people killed. She'd be better off trying to get information from the town librarian rather than the newspaper. She'd be able to answer questions, too.

Going to the pizza place in town around ten, she asked if they had any work for her. They usually did, and she was glad that she could work today. They never asked her for her phone number. Whenever she had free time, she would go in and ask. It was also a good way to hear things. She was hoping that the town would be abuzz about what had gone on at one of the biggest restaurants in town.

By the time her shift was over and she'd signed up for tomorrow too, she heard three different versions of what had happened at the *Golden Sheep.* She was going to have to get more information, but the police had made sure that no one could get into the parking lot, and there were no cameras around either.

The first version was that the place had blown up from a gas leak. She knew that one wasn't right. They never mentioned the dead bodies, nor did they talk about how the Feds were there either. It had been a big deal to have the Feds around because the owner had blown it up for tax purposes and insurance. She didn't believe that one to be true.

Nor did she think the second one she'd heard was true. It said that the gas leaked again, but since it didn't blow the place up, they only just had to evacuate. Again, no mention of bodies or dead people, so she didn't hold out much hope of that one being true either. She'd seen at least four of the dead and thought about number three. It had the most truth to it.

There was no gas leak, but it did mention that the place had been gone over by the Feds. It was said that Mr. Shadows had been arrested, but that was easy enough to get wrong. No one had seen his body as yet, and they were speculating on how he might have been taken out of the picture. It talked about how there were other agencies around and that they weren't allowing anyone within a mile of the place. The road had even been blocked off.

The thing was that she had it in her head that the place was selling some kind of illegal drugs. Whether it was fentanyl or not, she wasn't sure, but there was something going on. Just as she was clocking out of the pizza shop, they got a big order for ten large pizzas and five large salads. It could only be one family that ordered like that, and the Penningtons were not ones to mess with. They had a way about them that scared even her. Plus, they were big men who were soft-spoken. The kind of combination that would get a person into trouble with them. She stayed long enough to get the pizzas in the oven and the salads made. It was good money working for the town's only pizza place, and they were always busy.

~*~

Gleason and Raphael went in to get the pizzas. This was an unplanned dinner with the family, and he was glad that Creno's was able to accommodate them tonight. As soon as he picked up the salads, he could smell the pizzas cooking in the large oven. He loved hot pizza and loved it spicy as well. Creno's had the best hot and spicy around as far as he was concerned. Rapheal got half the pizza boxes, and he was going back in to get the rest of them.

"That girl is back working." He'd heard about the woman. Girl her family called her. She never stayed still long enough for them to get to know her, but he'd not seen a problem with it. Raphael thought that she was being suspicious, but he thought that she was just being cautious. "Don't you wonder where she came from? I do. I think she's being cagey when I've asked for her name, too. Most women are happy to give us their number."

"Maybe she just doesn't like you." Rapheal rolled his eyes. "Well, she might not. I've known a couple of women who think we're too cocky. Perhaps she's one of them."

"I'm not cocky, nor am I being paranoid. I've heard Kinsey say that about me and her." They put the pizzas in the back of the car and wrapped them up with the blanket that was forever in the back seat. When they were on their way, Raphael turned to look at him. "Have you ever noticed how she seems to disappear after a few comments to her? I think she's hiding from someone."

"I think you should just leave it alone." He wasn't going to, and he didn't waste his breath on her and him again. "What kind of pizzas did they get? I hope at least two of them are the hot and spicy. I'll have to fight Wylie for one if not. He loves them more than I do."

"They got three. Apparently, Rosie likes them spicy, too. I just like plain cheese when we're all together. I like my ice cream plain vanilla, too. I enjoy the simple things in life." Gleason decided there was no talking to some people, and Raphael was one of them. "I'm going to have Ara investigate her to see what's going on with her."

"Don't do it. You're just going to piss her off, and that won't be good. What if she's one of our soon-to-be wives? It won't be good family get-togethers if she's going to be pissed off at you all the time. No more pizzas either." He said he'd take his chances. "Besides,

Ara is trying to figure out what happened at the *Sheep*. He said that the county morgue was out there loading bodies when he tried to drive by."

"I've heard about that. They're not saying what happened there, but I'm to understand that the Feds have taken over the investigation. Whatever is going on, they sure have a lot of firepower out there. I had to turn around and go back the other way when I was headed to Columbus yesterday. They're not allowing anyone within a couple of miles of the place." Rapheal said he'd heard it was drugs. "I don't know why not. The couple of times I've been there, the parking lot looks full, but the restaurant is dead. Just me and another table. Could be that they're running drugs out of there from the basement."

"Yeah, I forgot it had a basement. Remember playing around the building when it was being renovated all those years ago?" He said that he did and then brought up the girl again. "I doubt very much she had anything to do with it. Whatever happened out there, it's going to come out that it was just a gas leak, and that will be the end of it."

"I don't know. Why would the Feds be out there if it were just a gas leak? I'm betting that they're making meth or something. Remember how we thought they were putting in a lot of heat for the place when we were screwing around? I think it might be drugs, and we're going to find out that the girl had something to do with it." He asked him when he'd gotten so paranoid before. "I'm not. I just read a lot of murder crime books. I'm reading one right now that talks about how this entire family was caught making meth in their basement. It wasn't until a cartel went in that they were found out. That's probably what happened out there."

"You need to get laid. At the very least, get out and date more. And quit reading those books. They're going to get your ass in trouble." They were home in a few minutes, but Raphael kept talking about the *Sheep*. He had the entire household talking about it while they got dinner. He was sure that they were all just humoring him, but he couldn't tell. Gleason just wanted to eat his pizza in peace and quiet. That wasn't going to happen with this family.

After dinner and clean up, they watched a preseason game on television. Wylie had the biggest television, so it was like being on the field with the players. Rosie knew a great deal about the game, so it was fun to watch her as well. The rest of them sat around the room, cursing and yelling.

By ten, they were hungry again. Since the pizza shop had closed at nine-thirty, they were out of options with the food. Mae, the cook, had been able to make them all subs, and it would tie them over until they got home. He wanted his spicy and wasn't really surprised when she was able to produce one hot enough for him. Rosie had her own special blend of the stuff, and he was going to have to get with her to get the recipe. It was too good to pass up.

As the game was winding down, he heard his brothers talking about the restaurant again. It was a big deal, and he understood the reason behind talking about it, but he was sick of it. And even if the girl had anything to do with it, she wasn't standing around talking about it all the time. She seemed to be just as quiet as she normally was when he saw her around town.

After making his way home, he decided that he needed something sweet. Pulling out the container of ice cream that he had, he was happy to see that there was just enough for him. Gleason really didn't like flavors either when it came to ice cream, but he would eat it if it was around. He liked his tea plain, too, and not flavored with things like pumpkin spice or oranges. If he wanted either, he'd cook something with it.

Going up to bed, he tried to remember if he'd had to work in the morning. He'd been hanging out at the feed store for the gossip and would be asked to help carry heavy loads of feed to the car. While he didn't need the money, they would usually pay him under the table, and he'd use that money to buy himself dinner somewhere. He enjoyed eating out more than he did cooking for one. It just wasn't any fun to cook, then clean up, too.

Getting ready for sleep, he picked up the book he'd been reading. It wasn't a murder crime novel like Raphael had been reading, but it held his interest. It was a book on investing and called *Investing for Dummies*. He didn't care what the title was; he was learning a great deal from it and would recommend it to anyone who was only just starting out in doing what the books suggested.

His cell phone was ringing when he was ready to turn out the light at eleven-thirty. It was his brother Raphael. He said that he'd had some news about the *Sheep*.

"I just read something on the internet. It says that there were fourteen people killed, and they're still looking for bodies. I guess the basement caught fire when there were shots fired, and the Feds are looking into a cartel that was pissed off about the restaurant making meth and selling it to their customer base." He asked him where he'd read that. "I swear it came from a good source."

"What source? Are you looking on the dark web again? I told you that it's going to get you into trouble. Do you want to spend the rest of your life in prison like Dad did? Just give it up. There isnt anything wrong with the place out there other than a few nutballs making shit up." He said that McGee was part of the cleanup. "Why would you believe that? We do have enough news going around now without making up things to go with our new chief of police."

"I tell you, Gleason, it's true. The web has witnesses out there who have seen the place. And you have to admit that it has some merit." He said he didn't have to admit anything of the sort. "You're just jealous because I was right. You'll see. It's going to come out that there are bodies everywhere and that it had to do with meth being made on the premises. I'm going to see if I can get into the place to see what's going on."

"It's your funeral, dumbass." He wondered if Raphael would really do it and decided that he would. "Don't go out there. If it is what you say, then they're not going to take too lightly that someone is sneaking around the property and getting caught. I'm sure that there have been people who have been caught doing the same thing and are right now in a federal prison. You can't be serious about trying to get there."

"I'm not stupid." He let go of the breath he'd been holding, thinking he wasn't sure about his brother right now. "I'm not going to go out there other than to drive by. Just to see what's going on. There has to be something. Why would they still have the road closed off if there was nothing going on? Answer me that."

"I don't know." He really didn't, but he didn't

think it had to do with meth. They were a small town, and that sort of thing never happened in small towns. Or did it? He didn't know, but he was sure that Raphael was going to get his ass in trouble if he didn't leave this alone. "What about talking to McGee? He might be able to tell you something. I don't know that I like him all that much, but he might have answers if you were to catch him in his office. I'll even go with you."

"Great. Tomorrow morning, then. We'll go to the police station and ask him point-blank what's going on. We as citizens of this town have a right to know, don't you think?" He didn't know what to think, but he figured that if McGee knew anything, they'd be able to get it out of him. He wished that Rosie were still chief; she'd be able to tell them everything that they wanted to know. He had a feeling, however, that she was just as much in the dark as they were. "We'll get to him before he leaves for the day. He's not been in his office for the last few days. I'm betting that he knows something. I mean, it did happen on his watch."

"I'm going to ban you from reading period if you don't stop with the murder crime books. You're becoming as bad as some of those people under the bridge in Zanesville. You know the ones, they push around shopping carts all over looking for bottles to cash in." Raphael said that he wasn't that bad and that he was right. "Right or not, you're going to get your ass in trouble if you keep this up. We both know that you can take things a little overboard sometimes."

"I'll show you. I was right about that girl from high school, too. She was pregnant." She had been, and it had been all over school that her father had been the father. Turned out that Raphael had been right in that it had been her uncle and that the uncle had gone to prison for a long time when he'd killed her because she told someone that she was going to have his baby. That had been at least fifteen years ago now. "I'll see you in the morning. You'll see. I'm right about this. I've put a lot of effort into figuring it out."

He really had, and that was the scary part. Gleason always thought that Raphael should write books he had read so many. And murder crime had been the one that he usually read.

Chapter 10

Wylie watched his brothers walk into the jail. He did wonder what was going on, but didn't bother them. He was on a stakeout with Rosie, and she was watching the jail too. She turned to look at him when he said her name.

"I wonder what they're doing in there?" He said they were no doubt causing trouble. Not the serious kind, but enough to have tongues wagging. "McGee hasn't left yet. He's been consistent in leaving every day at eight on the dot. Do you suppose he had an appointment with your brothers?"

"I doubt he'd wait around on them if he knew they were coming in. Gleason doesn't look happy about something, and Raphael looks like he knows something. Do you suppose he's going in there to ask about the *Sheep*? That's all he could talk about last night when he was over to the house."

"He's guessing really well. My source tells me that there were fourteen bodies from the lower levels of the place and five from the kitchen. The other drug dealers came in, firing up the place and killing whoever got in their way." He couldn't believe that it had happened nearly at their front door. "I guess they were in on their territory, and that pissed them off. It was a good plan to have them make meth in a restaurant. No one would be suspicious about a high gas bill when they were cooking food. However, they got caught, and that's not a good thing for around here. They'll be speculating on it for years to come if it doesn't get leaked out of the jail sooner rather than later."

"I'm thinking that they're just lucky that so few had been killed. If the place had been full of dining customers, there is no telling what the body count would have been." She agreed with him. Then she noticed that Gleason and Raphael were being escorted out. "That can't be good. I wonder what they did to have that happen. I've never had to escort anyone out of the jail before. I've wanted to, but it seemed to be too much effort to do that instead of letting them leave on their own."

"I'm betting it has to do with Raphael. He's got a burr up his ass about the restaurant, and he won't leave it alone, no matter how many times he's been told not to bother. It will just make him dig his heels in deeper until he gets himself hurt. Or someone else." He pointed to the station house. "Look, there goes McGee. What makes you so sure that he's working with the Feds on this?"

"He is. They said that while he's not in charge,

he's making enough of a nuisance about himself that they're letting him hang around." Rosie started the car. "We can only follow him so far, then he'll turn into the drive that leads to the parking lot. If they wanted to make it so no one cared about what was going on, they shouldn't have done that. I would have just kept the house out of sight. They could do that with a couple of well-placed tents."

He didn't care if he got any information about what had happened. He was just enjoying himself getting to do this with Rosie. She'd gotten a call in the middle of the night about what had really happened at the place and how meth had been being made on the premises. It wasn't until an hour later that she was called again to say that Mr. Shadows had been killed along with his wife and daughter. They'd been the ones who were running the operations and had been killed terribly. There had been a dishwasher who had been killed along with one of the waitstaff. It was a bloody mess out there, and he wondered if they'd ever find the ones that had done the killing.

McGee had been the first one on sight, and he'd been in charge of the operations long enough for some of the other staff to have been let go. The feds were looking for any information about the people, and he knew from Rosie that it had been two men and two women. They'd all been in the kitchen staff when things went off, and now they didn't know where to find them.

"Wouldn't they have been able to find them with the information that was on their driver's license?" Wylie thought that was what he'd seen done in the movies. They took down their information so they'd have it for later. "I mean, that's what I would have done before I let them go."

"Apparently, it was done, but now they can't find it. I don't know why, but I think that McGee has it on his person and is keeping it hidden away so that he can be the big hero and get things going. I wouldn't put it past him." He'd not met the guy for very long, but he really didn't care for him. He was slick, like someone would think a car salesman would be. He didn't know any slick car salesmen, but he knew the reference. "I'm betting right now it's in the safe in the office, with not just the names of the people that he let go but some of the evidence too. He's a cocky son of a bitch."

They followed McGee all the way out to the *Sheep.* Once they were at a point where they could see the place, they were stopped and told to turn around. She did so without complaint to the man, but cursed him all the way home. It was funny to him that his little wife had such a vocabulary of words that weren't fit for company. He asked her if he could drive home, and she stomped around the car to the passenger side. He had to bite his tongue or laugh out loud when she got in and slammed the door.

"I don't understand what the big deal is. Just tell the public what happened and be done with it. They certainly wouldn't have to have all this extra intrigue or anything. Just post signs saying that there was no trespassing, and that would be the end of it." Rosie told him he was being naïve.

"People would want to go in and see for themselves what a drug ring looked like. They might even steal something, like I know McGee did, to make it so that the case is never solved. Then what do you do if someone gets hurt trespassing? It could happen, and they'd sue them for not having enough barriers up, even though they'd been told to stay out. I know people. They're okay when they're alone, but get a group of them together, and Armageddon will come around."

He could see that. His grannie used to say something like that all the time when she'd been alive. That one person was smart, and that a group of smart people suddenly became stupid. He never really believed it until today.

Since she knew that McGee was gone for the day, she wanted him to drop her off at the stationhouse. She didn't think she'd get any more information than her snitch was telling her, but she said it was worth a try.

What pissed her off the most was that had she waited one more day to retire, she would have been in charge of the operation, and the number of things that she'd done differently would have had the case solved by now. Not really, but he wanted to think that she could solve anything given enough information.

After dropping her off, he went home. They were expecting a delivery today, and he would have to sign for it. It was some of the kitchen aides that they decided they needed, but not right away. Ordering through an online store got it to them in a couple of days instead of having to travel all the way to Columbus again. He loved ordering online.

No crowds of people. No driving. He was even happy to pay for shipping because he knew that he'd spend more than that on gas. There wasn't even any kind of hassle when he had to return it for some reason. Just print out a label and take it to another store, and there it was. Done and done. He would even get his refund back before he left the parking lot on some days. Since he relied on reviews, he always left one so that the next person would know what sort of issues or not that he'd had.

~*~

Rosie didn't get any information from the stationhouse, but she did have fun. They'd missed her they told her, and her ways of doing things. She did notice that a couple of people asked her when she was coming back to work, had she found retirement just too boring. She told them that she was enjoying her new life and couldn't wait until the holidays so that she could get into them more than she had any other year before.

She'd only been gone a few days, but it did seem longer to her. Not having to get up every day was nice and wearing the bulky uniform wasn't something that she was going to miss either. For now, she was enjoying her lazy days off and deciding on the nursery things they had to sort through online.

Getting ready to leave when they were called out on a call, she was asked if she knew anything about the Golden Sheep. Shaking her head no, because she couldn't say anything different, she told them that she'd tried to go out that way to get some things from Columbus and had had to turn around and go back.

"I guess it's a big to-do out there. We're kept in the dark, too, about it. The only thing we know for sure is that McGee goes out there daily to have a look around. We don't know what he's looking for, but he seems to think they can't run the thing without his input." The officer laughed. "Are you sure you don't want to come out of retirement for us? I sure do miss you being behind the desk. As it is now, we have to call him on the cell phone, and he sometimes doesn't answer. Too busy, I guess."

"I know that the place was blown up." He said that they heard that only a small portion of it had caught fire, and there were dead people still lying about up there. "I doubt that much. I mean, they would have had to have done a mortem on them by now, don't you think?"

"I thought of that too." She asked him why he hadn't asked McGee. "He said that we were on a need-to-know basis and that we didn't need to know until he told us. I don't know. It sounds to me like it's a drug deal that went bad. Why have all those Feds out there if there is nothing but a murder going on? That's what we've put together anyway. That it was some kind of murder that had killed a few people, and they're making a Federal case out of it for some reason."

She went home feeling more frustrated than she had this morning when she'd left to follow McGee. She didn't know how he expected his officers to help him if he was keeping them in the dark, too. Itching to know more, she laid down on the couch at home to wait for Wylie to get home. He wasn't due until four o'clock this afternoon, after traveling back and forth to help her out.

He'd been working for Meggie for the past few days. He told her that he didn't know what he was doing, but would try to sort out some information for her since she was paying him to do that. He was currently on a farm in Tennessee that was looking to expand their cattle. While he knew about cattle on some level, he didn't know a great deal about land deals. This was a sort of learn as he went situation. She remembered the conversation from last night before going to bed.

"She wants to know if there is enough land for them to have as many cattle as they want. I did a search on it and found out how many heads you should have per acre. After that, it's a simple thing to multiply the number of acres you have by the number of cattle you can have on each part. He's way over the limit now for the well-being of the cattle that he has." She asked him if he told Meggie. "I did, and the man. He seems to think that the amount is all screwed up somehow and that he knows better than anyone else."

"What did Meggie say?" He told her that she wasn't going to lend him the money unless he bought more land. And it was available for him to purchase around where he lived. "That's good. I'm glad that she's taking what I told her seriously. I'd hate to think what would happen to the cattle if they're crowded too much. There wouldn't be enough land to graze on for them, and that could cause starvation."

He had left for Meggie's office after dropping her off at the station house, and she was looking forward to what else she had to say about the farm and the cattle. She'd do her own research, too, but it was nice having someone who worked for her to have insider knowledge on the way things worked. Even if he did have to look it up to know for sure.

She dozed off and on while lying there. Getting up at around noon to have lunch, she was back on the couch lying down. She wasn't lazy, she didn't think, but she'd been working for so long and hard at it that she felt like her body was catching up on what it had missed out on for so many years.

Waking up at around two, she got up to go to the bathroom. After washing her hands, she decided that she'd rested long enough and went to her makeshift office to work on the things that Meggie had her doing. It wasn't much more than just going over the notes on her security team, but it was enough to keep her busy and her mind working. As soon as she turned off the computer and wandered around the house for a bit, she knew that she was going to have to find herself something to do, or she was going to be resting all day and never get anything done.

Pulling up the want ads in the newspaper, she found that they were hiring at the pizza shop in town. She thought that she might enjoy that a couple of days a week and decided to apply. They were holding open interviews today, and she got dressed to go and see if she could work there. It would be a great way to stay connected with the town and keep her from sitting around the house all day like a couch potato.

There wasn't anyone there when she arrived, and she thought that was odd. There seemed to be a lot of people out of work around town, and she thought that they'd jump at the opportunity to have a job. She didn't need the money, but she did need something to do while she was retired from the police force.

While she was waiting for the manager for her interview, she watched the people behind the lines. There was one girl there who seemed to be too shy to interact with people, but she seemed to be good at her job. As she watched her making a pizza, she wondered how many of the pizzas that they'd had over the past month that she'd made for them.

The interview went well, and it didn't surprise her at all that the manager, Kyle, asked her if she could work tomorrow's lunchtime shift. He said that it was busy, but it was a good time to start to see if she was going to like it or not. She didn't think she'd have any trouble, so she was glad that she was going to be able to start so soon. Working somewhere was better than not, and she was happy for the opportunity to have a job that worked with her schedule.

She told Wylie all about her job when he got home, and he was happy for her. Explaining to him about how she didn't want to stay at home all day, he agreed with her. He said that he'd been having the same trouble too and that he thought being wealthy had its drawbacks. Like having nothing to do was big on his list, too.

After dinner, the two of them watched some preseason football. It wasn't the same without his family around, but they yelled at the referees as much as they did the players. It was a fun evening, and by ten o'clock, they were both ready for bed. As they were headed up to their bedroom, she told him about her job and what it would entail, and he asked her if she got a discount.

"I didn't ask. I would think so, but now when we all get together. I'd hate for them to lose money on hiring me." Wylie said he'd been kidding, and they both laughed. "I'll find out tomorrow. I'm excited to be able to work during such a busy time for them. It'll make the day go by so much faster than sitting around here all day with nothing to do. Did I tell you about the stationhouse?"

Telling him about the officers who had worked for her made her feel so good about wanting her to come back that she got a little teary-eyed. She wasn't as touchy as Meggie had been about things, but sometimes when it hit her really hard, at times, she couldn't help but cry. It was her emotions all over the place that exhausted her. She thought that having a baby was hard on a woman and wondered why people had them. Then she'd remember that it was Wylie's baby, and that made everything worthwhile to her.

Getting up the next morning, she was ready to go by ten-thirty. She was told to wear jeans and a T-shirt, and they'd give her a shirt when she got there. She was going to watch for the first few days in order to see how they made their food. Excited to be able to be out of the house, she paid attention to what was going on and enjoyed watching the food come together. She thought that she could work here full-time and never get bored.

By three o'clock, she was wondering about her life choices. Standing on her feet all day had taken its toll on her lower back, and her feet hurt. She'd had fun, that was sure, and she'd been greeted by a lot of people that she'd worked with, and that had been nice.

Walking home, she felt better to be out of the pizza place and out in the sunshine. Fall was coming up on them soon, and she could already see the trees turning. Fall and spring were her favorite times of the year, and she was looking forward to spending as much time outdoors as she could this year. Working all the time had taken that from her, and she was happy to be able to be out and about, too. Life was suddenly better than it had been in her life, and she knew that it had to do with having Wylie in her life.

Since she was sure she smelled like subs, she took a shower and washed her clothes. Washing her hair twice to get the smell out of it, she felt like she could eat dinner as soon as Wylie was home. He'd had another meeting with Meggie's team, and that had taken him most of the morning. Just as she was getting herself a snack for something to eat, she heard from Wylie.

"I'm going to pick you up here in about half an hour, and we're going to have dinner out. I don't even care if it's burgers someplace. I've had a wonderful day and want to share it with you." She grinned, thinking that he was in a good mood. "I get paid on Friday, and Meggie was telling me that since I'd saved her a great deal of money, I get a bonus. I'm all for bonuses even if it's only twenty bucks."

"I know what you mean. I got to make my first pizza today, and I didn't mess it up. Even when it came out of the oven, I was proud of it so much that I took a picture. Of course, everyone teased me about it, but I don't care. I had a wonderful day too. Except that my feet hurt. I'm going to have to get myself some different shoes." He told her that he was proud of her, too, and asked her to send him the picture. He was going to use it for his homepage so that he could see her pizza all the time. "You're being goofy now. I love you for it, however. Thanks. I'll send it to you now."

She did that and laughed when he told her that it was the best-looking pizza that he'd ever seen. He went on and on about it for so long that she was a little embarrassed. Once he said that he was coming home, she decided to get dressed up for dinner, even as he said it was just burgers. She wanted to feel pretty today and was happy that he was excited about his job as well.

They ended up going to their favorite place. The seafood was always delicious, and they usually got good service. Tonight was no different in that they had a good time and were stuffed by the time they were finished. Neither of them wanted dessert, but they did decide to walk around again and found a little bookstore that had all kinds of genres they read. He ended up buying three books he'd wanted to read, and she found two that she'd been reading from his library that were the next in the series.

Walking back to their car, they talked about reading books. Most people they had surmised used readers, but the two of them liked reading a book with pages to turn and the smell of the printed word. Getting into the car, they kissed, and she asked him what that was for.

"For being who you are." He started the car, and they were off. "I've been thinking about a way to tell our family that we're going to have a baby. I'm sure that you want to tell your parents too, so why don't we get them all together for a dinner party and tell them then? Not right away, but in a few weeks. After everything with our jobs has settled down."

"I love that idea. Mom has been hinting like crazy that she wants to be a grandma. I didn't tell her anything, but it's fun knowing something that she doesn't. It's going to be fun when we tell them all at one time." He said that he could plan the party and they'd not have to do anything, as they'd have it catered. "I love that idea too. They'll even do the cleanup, and that will be nice for the staff. It's nice having the money to do that, but I'd not want to do it all the time. That could be really expensive."

"This is a special occasion and should be fun." She agreed with him and decided they'd have something to do with seafood, too. "I like that. I think that most of my brothers like seafood, and it would be fun to get them all together to have some. We could even have some steaks on the grill to have a good variety."

She did wonder what it was going to cost and decided that she didn't care. It was a celebration, and they should go all out. As soon as they were home, she decided that she was too tired to stay up late and headed up to bed. When Wylie joined her in the bedroom, she asked him if he was all right.

"I heard from my brothers. They tried to get to McGee to see what was going on out at the *Sheep*. Apparently, they didn't have any more luck than you did. But they did get a little information about the people who had been killed. They know now that at least twenty have been killed, and there are still the missing employees. They seem to think that it's the woman at the pizza shop. Don't ask me why they think that. I don't understand any more than I could explain it to you." He laughed. "I don't know that the two of them should be hanging out together. They seem to have trouble following them around. And if that's not happening, they make trouble when there is no reason to. They've been like that since they were kids. Also, Raphael thinks that the girl I was talking about is in on the cover-up somehow and that she's going to be a key witness in what's going on out there. I have no idea where they come up with their theories."

She was still smiling when she closed her eyes. Tomorrow she had to work again and was looking forward to it. While out tonight, she'd picked herself up some tennis shoes that she could wear to work and was happy that she'd remembered the name brand of the ones that most of the staff wore. Perhaps she'd make a sub tomorrow and be ready to take on orders for herself. She was looking forward to becoming reliable for them and was happy that she'd applied for the job. It was going to be fun getting out of the house from now on, and she didn't care that she didn't need the money.

Awake at seven, she was getting dressed when she heard from her mom. She wanted to have lunch tomorrow, and she didn't have to work. After telling her about her job, her mother tsked at her about taking jobs from those who needed them, and she explained that no one else had come in to apply for the job, so she got it.

"I hope you're only working part-time." She said that she was only working a couple of days a week. "That's good. Now that you're not working for the department, we can have lunch more often instead of being on a time constraint because you have to get back to work. I'm going to love being around you more often."

"I'd like that as well. I'm only working to get out of the house. I don't want to have lunch with you every day, but a couple of times would be great. I miss you too." Her mom said she wasn't getting any younger and didn't want to waste time without seeing her only child. "Don't talk like that. You're young yet, and I'm not going to think about you dying today. I'm having a wonderful day—I got to talk to you, so don't talk about dying right now."

"I'm sorry. A friend of mine's daughter was

killed in a car accident this morning. Someone ran a stop sign, and when she tried to avoid it, the police said that she hit another car head-on. She was declared dead at the scene." She told her that she was sorry, and she was. Especially when she heard that she was only thirty-one years old. "Such a waste of life. She had so much going for her that my heart breaks for her husband. They didn't have any kids, but they'd only been married for a few years."

"I'm going to change the subject now. I hope that's all right. I don't want to talk about people dying anymore." She said she was sorry. "Don't be. I just hurt for them too, and I didn't even know them. I'm looking forward to having lunch with you tomorrow, and we'll talk about fun things. Maybe we can get a little shopping done. I have a few things on my list that we still need for the house. Would you mind going with me to get them?"

"I'd love to spend more time with you. Yes, I'll be happy to join you. I have a few things on my list as well. Perhaps you can not buy all of it, and I can get you something for Christmas. I'm guessing that you and Wylie will have a large tree since this is your first holiday together." She said they'd not talked about it. "It won't be long now. The leaves are changing, and before you know it, it'll be Thanksgiving again. That's my favorite holiday. Please say that you'll make some time to come to our house that day. I'd miss you if you didn't."

"I don't know what the plans are. Since I'm new to the family, I'm playing it by ear this time. Maybe we could have you guys over with his family. I think that Kinsey and Meggie are going all out this year, too." She said that she'd miss cooking but was looking forward to whatever she wanted her to do. "Thanks, Mom. I love you."

"I love you too, darling." She laughed a little, and it made her smile. "I was just thinking that it would be a good time to tell us all that you're expecting. I know that Meggie is now, and when I saw her in town the other day, I would swear that she was glowing. I'd love to have a baby around to spoil for the holidays."

"We've only been married for a few months. Sheesh, Mom, give it some time. I just retired from the police force." She said that she knew but could hope for it. "You keep on hoping, and I'll see what I can do."

After getting off the phone with her mom, she made her way to work. It was going to be a good day today, she could just feel it in her bones. She'd work hard and be able to hold her head up high when, at the end of the day, she'd learned something. And she was planning on learning a great deal with her new job and was going to have fun while she was at it.

Before You Go...

HELP AN AUTHOR

write a review

THANK YOU!

Share your voice and help guide other readers to these wonderful books. Even if it's only a line or two, your reviews help readers discover the author's books so they can continue creating stories that you'll love. Log in to your favorite retailer and leave a review. Thank you.

AWARD WINNING, BESTSELLING AUTHOR

Kathi S. Barton is an award-winning and bestselling author known for her steamy paranormal romances and unforgettable characters. A recipient of the prestigious Pinnacle Book Achievement Award, her books have topped the charts on Amazon and All Romance eBooks, earning her a loyal global readership.

Kathi lives in Nashport, Ohio, with her husband, Paul. When she's not crafting passionate love stories set in magical worlds, she enjoys camping, exploring local auctions, and attending county fairs, where Paul showcases his artwork and pottery. Her creative spark—fueled by a muse she describes as a cross between Jimmy Stewart and Hugh Jackman—brings her stories to vivid, heartfelt life.

Paranormal romance with plenty of heat is her favorite genre, and she loves connecting with her readers. Feel free to reach out— Kathi would love to hear from you.

Email: aaronskiss@gmail.comFollow Kathi on her blog: http://kathisbartonauthor.blogspot.com/